D1013545

SPACE WAR!

The Sirian's lips stretched into a humorless smile. "In recent weeks Earth has called an interstellar conference to consider what they chose to call our invasion of their territory. You will testify that Earth attacked first!"

"I cannot testify to what is not the truth," Lucky Starr answered.

The Sirian's eyes narrowed to slits. "I think you will. You have been studied closely by our agents, and we know of the Council of Science's sentiment for the weak. Testify or your engineer will die!"

ISAAC ASIMOV

writing as Paul French

LUCKY STARR

and

THE RINGS OF SATURN

A FAWCETT CREST BOOK

Fawcett Books, Greenwich, Connecticut

LUCKY STARR AND THE RINGS OF SATURN

THIS BOOK CONTAINS THE COMPLETE TEXT OF
THE ORIGINAL HARDCOVER EDITION.

Published by Fawcett Crest Books, CBS Publications, CBS
Consumer Publishing, a division of CBS, Inc., by arrangement with Doubleday and Company, Inc.

ISBN: 0-449-23462-2

Printed in the United States of America

10 9 8 7 6 5 4 3 2 1

CONTENTS

DEDICATION

To the memory of
Henry Kuttner
and
Cyril Kornbluth

Preface

Back in the 1950s, I wrote a series of six derring-do novels about David "Lucky" Starr and his battles against malefactors within the Solar System. Each of the six took place in a different region of the system, and in each case I made use of the astronomical facts—as they were then known.

Now, a quarter-century later, Fawcett is bringing out the novels in new editions; but what a quarter-century it has been! More has been learned about the worlds of our Solar System in this last quarter-century than in all the thousands of years that went before.

LUCKY STARR AND THE RINGS OF SATURN was written in 1957, but in 1967, a French astronomer, Audouin Dollfus, discovered a tenth satellite of Saturn, one that was closer to the planet than any of the others, 22,000 miles closer to Saturn than Mimas is. This new satellite has been named Janus.

If I were writing the book today, I would certainly mention that satellite and I might have used it instead of Mimas.

Moreover, it was not until 1977 that astronomers discovered that Saturn was not the only ringed planet. Uranus, it turns out, also has rings. They are very thin rings and very faint ones—but they're there. I would surely have mentioned that in this book if I were writing it today.

I hope my Gentle Readers enjoy the book anyway, as an adventure story, but please don't forget that the advance of science can outdate even the most conscientious science-fiction writer and that my astronomical descriptions are no longer accurate in all respects.

ISAAC ASIMOV

1

The Invaders

The Sun was a brilliant diamond in the sky, just large enough to the naked eye to be made out as something more than a star; as a tiny white-hot pea-sized globe.

Out here in the vastness of space, near the second largest planet of the Solar System, the Sun gave out only one per cent of the light it cast on man's home planet. It was still, however, the brightest object in the sky, as four thousand full Moons would be.

Lucky Starr gazed thoughtfully at the visiplate which centered the image of the distant Sun. John Bigman Jones watched with him, an odd contrast to Lucky's tall and rangy figure. When John Bigman Jones stretched himself to his full height, he stood five foot two exactly. But the little man did not measure himself in inches and he allowed people to call him by his middle name only: Bigman.

Bigman said, "You know, Lucky, it's nearly nine hundred million miles away. The Sun, I mean. I've never been out this far."

The third man in the cabin, Councilman Ben Wessilewsky, grinned over his shoulder from his place at the controls. He was another large man, though not as tall as Lucky, and his shock of yellow hair topped

a face that had grown space-brown in the service of
the Council of Science.

He said, "What's the matter, Bigman? Scared way
out here?"

Bigman squawked, "Sands of Mars, Wess, you get
your hands off those controls and say that again."

He had dodged around Lucky and was making for
the Councilman, when Lucky's hands came down
on Bigman's shoulders and lifted him bodily. Bigman's legs still pumped, as though carrying him
toward Wess at a charge, but Lucky put his Mars-born
friend back in his original position.

"Stay put, Bigman."

"But, Lucky, you heard him. This long cobber
thinks there's more *to* a man just because there's
more *of* him. If that Wess is six feet tall, that just
means there's an extra foot of flab——"

"All right, Bigman," said Lucky. "And, Wess, let's
save the humor for the Sirians."

He spoke quietly to both, but there was no questioning his authority.

Bigman cleared his throat and said, "Where's
Mars?"

"On the other side of the Sun from us."

"Wouldn't you know," said the little fellow dis-
gustedly. Then, brightening, "But hold on, Lucky,
we're a hundred million miles below the plane of
the Ecliptic. We ought to be able to see Mars below
the Sun; peeking out from behind, sort of."

"Uh-huh, we should. Actually, it's a degree or so
away from the Sun, but that's close enough for it
to be drowned out in the glare. You can make out
Earth, though, I think."

Bigman allowed a look of haughty disgust to cross his face. "Who in space wants to see Earth? There isn't anything there but people; mostly groundhogs who've never even been a hundred miles off the surface. I wouldn't look at it if that were all there was in the sky to look at. You let Wess look at it. That's his speed."

He walked moodily away from the visiplate.

Wess said, "Hey, Lucky, how about getting Saturn on and taking a good look at it from this angle? Come on, I've been promising myself a treat."

"I don't know," said Lucky, "that the sight of Saturn these days is exactly what you might call a treat."

He said it lightly, but for a moment silence fell uneasily within the confined pilot room of *The Shooting Starr*.

All three felt the change in atmosphere. Saturn meant danger. Saturn had taken on a new face of doom to the peoples of the Terrestrial Federation. To six billion people on Earth, to additional millions on Mars, the Moon, and Venus, to scientific stations on Mercury, Ceres, and the outer moons of Jupiter, Saturn had become something newly and unexpectedly deadly.

Lucky was the first to shrug off that moment of depression, and, obedient to the touch of his fingers, the sensitive electronic scanners set into the hull of *The Shooting Starr* rotated smoothly on their universal gimbals. As that happened, the field of vision in the visiplate shifted.

The stars marched across the visiplate in steady

procession, and Bigman said with a curl of hatred in his upper lip, "Any of those things Sirius, Lucky?"

"No," said Lucky, "we're working through the Southern Celestial Hemisphere and Sirius is in the Northern. Would you like to see Canopus?"

"No," said Bigman. "Why should I?"

"I just thought you might be interested. It's the second brightest star and you could pretend it was Sirius." Lucky smiled slightly. It always amused him that the patriotic Bigman should be so annoyed because Sirius, home star of the great enemies of the Solar System (though themselves descendants of Earthmen), was the brightest star in Earth's heavens.

Bigman said, "Very funny. Come on, Lucky, let's see Saturn, and then when we get back to Earth you can get on some comedy show and panic everybody."

The stars kept their smooth motion, then slowed and stopped. Lucky said, "There it is—unmagnified, too."

Wess locked the controls and twirled in the pilot's seat so that he might see also.

It was a half-moon in appearance, somewhat bulging into more than half, just large enough to be seen as such, bright with a soft yellow light that was dimmer in the center than along the edges.

"How far away are we?" Bigman asked in astonishment.

Lucky said, "About a hundred million miles, I think."

"Something's wrong," Bigman said. "Where are the rings? I've been counting on a good look."

The Shooting Starr was high above the south pole of

Saturn. From that position it should see the rings broad on.

Lucky said, "The rings are blurred into the globe of the planet, Bigman, because of the distance. Suppose we magnify the image and take a closer look."

The spot of light that was Saturn expanded and stretched in every direction, growing. And the half-moon that it had seemed to be broke up into three segments.

There was still a central globe, half-mooned. Around it, however, touching the globe at no point, was a circularly curved ribbon of light, divided into two unequal halves by a dark line. As the ribbon curved about Saturn and entered its shadow, it was cut off in darkness.

"Yes, sir, Bigman," said Wess, lecturing, "Saturn itself is only seventy-eight thousand miles in diameter. At a hundred million miles, it would just be a dot of light, but count in the rings and there are nearly two hundred thousand miles of reflecting surface from one end to the other."

"I know all that," said Bigman indignantly.

"And what's more," continued Wess, unheeding, "at a hundred million miles, the seven-thousand-mile break between Saturn's surface and the innermost portion of the rings just couldn't be seen; let alone the twenty-five-hundred-mile break that divides the rings in two. That black line is called Cassini's division, you know, Bigman."

"I said I know," roared Bigman. "Listen, Lucky, that cobber is trying to make out I didn't go to school. Maybe I didn't get much schooling, but there isn't anything he has to tell me about space. Say the word, Lucky; say you'll let him stop hiding behind you and I'll squash him like a bug."

Lucky said, "You can make out Titan."

At once Bigman and Wess said in chorus, "Where?"

"Right there." Titan showed as a tiny half-moon about the size, under current magnification, that Saturn and its ring system had appeared to be without magnification. It was near the edge of the visiplate.

Titan was the only sizable moon in the Saturnian system. But it wasn't its size that made Wess stare at it with curiosity and Bigman with hate.

It was, instead, that the three were almost certain that Titan was the only world in the Solar System populated by men who did not acknowledge the overlordship of Earth. Suddenly and unexpectedly it had been revealed as a world of the enemy.

It brought the danger suddenly closer. "When do we get inside the Saturnian system, Lucky?"

Lucky said, "There's no real definition as to what is the Saturnian system, Bigman. Most people consider a world's system to include all the space out to the distance where the farthermost body is moving under the gravitational influence of that world. If that's so, we're still outside the Saturnian system."

"The Sirians say, though——" began Wess.

"To Sun-center with the Sirian cobbers!" roared Bigman, slapping his high boots in anger. "Who cares what they say?" He slapped his boots again as though every Sirian in the system were under the force of his blows. His boots were the most truly Martian thing about him. Their raucous coloring, orange and black in a curving checkerboard design, was the loud proclamation that their owner had been born and bred among the Martian farms and domed cities.

Lucky blanked out the visiplate. The detectors on the ship's hulls retracted, leaving the ship's outer skin smooth, gleaming, and unbroken except for the bulge that ringed the stern and held *The Shooting Starr's* Agrav* attachment.

Lucky said, "We can't allow ourselves the luxury of the who-cares-what-they-say attitude, Bigman. At the moment the Sirians have the upper hand. Maybe we'll get them out of the Solar System eventually, but right now the only thing we can do is to play it their way for the while."

Bigman muttered rebelliously, "We're in our own system."

"Sure, but Sirius is occupying this part of it and, pending an interstellar conference, there isn't anything Earth can do about it, unless it's willing to start a war."

There was nothing to be said to that. Wess returned to his controls, and *The Shooting Starr,* with minimum expenditure of thrust, making use of Saturn's gravity to the maximum, continued to sink rapidly toward the polar regions of the planet.

Down, down, deeper into the grip of what was now a Sirian world, its space swarming with Sirian ships some fifty trillion miles from their home planet and only seven hundred million miles from Earth. In one giant step Sirius had covered 99.999 per cent of the distance between itself and Earth and established a military base on Earth's very doorstep.

* *Lucky Starr and the Moons of Jupiter.*

If Sirius were allowed to remain there, then in one sudden moment Earth would sink to the status of second-class power at Sirius's mercy. And the interstellar political situation was such that for the moment all of Earth's giant military establishment, all of her mighty ships and weapons were helpless to deal with the situation.

Only three men in one small ship, on their own initiative and unauthorized by Earth, were left to try, by skill and craft, to reverse the situation, knowing that if they were caught they could be executed out of hand as spies—in their own Solar System by invaders of that Solar System—and that Earth could not do a solitary thing to save them.

2

Pursuit

As little as a month ago there had been no thought of the danger, no barest notion, until it exploded in the face of Earth's government. Steadily and methodically the Council of Science had been cleaning up the nest of robot spies that had riddled Earth and its possessions and whose power had been broken by Lucky Starr on the snows of Io.*

It had been a grim job and, in a way, a frightening one, for the espionage had been thorough and efficient and, moreover, had come within an ace of succeeding and damaging Earth desperately.

Then, at the moment when the situation seemed completely in the clear at last, a crack appeared in the healing structure, and Hector Conway, Chief Councilman, awakened Lucky in the small hours one night. He showed signs of hurried dressing, and his fine white hair was in rumpled disarray.

Lucky, blinking sleep out of his eyes, offered coffee and said in amazement, "Great Galaxy, Uncle Hector" (Lucky had called him that since his early orphaned days, when Conway and Augustus Henree

* *Lucky Starr and the Moons of Jupiter.*

had been his guardians), "are the visiphone circuits out?"

"I dared not trust the visiphone, my boy. We're in a dreadful mess."

"In what way?" Lucky asked the question quietly, but he removed the upper half of his pajamas and began washing.

Bigman came in, stretching and yawning. "Hey, what's all this Mars-forsaken noise about?" Recognizing the Chief Councilman, he snapped into wakefulness. "Trouble, sir?"

"We've let Agent X slip through our fingers."

"Agent X? The mysterious Sirian?" Lucky's eyes narrowed a bit. "The last I heard of him, the Council had decided he didn't exist."

"That was before the robot spy business turned up. He's been clever, Lucky, darned clever. It takes a clever spy to convince the Council he doesn't exist. I should have put you on his track, but there always seemed something else you had to do. Anyway——"

"Yes?"

"You know how all this robot spy business showed there must be a central clearing agency for the information being gathered and that it pointed to a position on Earth itself as the location of the agency. That got us on the trail of Agent X all over again, and one of the strong possibilities for that role was a man named Jack Dorrance at Acme Air Products right here in International City."

"I hadn't known this."

"There were many other candidates for the job. But then Dorrance took a private ship off Earth and blasted right through an emergency block. It was a stroke of luck we had a Councilman at Port Center who took the right action at once and followed. Once the report of the ship's block-blasting reached us, it took only minutes to find that of all the suspects only Dorrance was out of surveillance check. He'd gotten past us. A few other matters fit in then and—anyway, he's Agent X. We're sure of it now."

"Very well, then, Uncle Hector. Where's the harm? He's gone."

"We know one more thing now. He's taken a personal capsule with him, and we have no doubt that that capsule contains information he has managed to collect from the spy network over the Federation, and, presumably, has not yet had time to deliver to his Sirian bosses. Space knows exactly what he has, but there must be enough there to blow our security to pieces if it gets into Sirian hands."

"You say he was followed. He has been brought back?"

"No." The harassed Chief Councilman turned pettish. "Would I be here if he had been?"

Lucky asked suddenly, "Is the ship he took equipped to make the Jump?"

"No," cried the ruddy-faced Chief Councilman, and he smoothed his silvered thatch of hair as though it had risen in horror at the very thought of the Jump.

Lucky drew a deep breath of relief too. The Jump was, of course, the leap through hyperspace, a movement that carried a ship outside ordinary space and brought it back again into a point in space many light-years away, all in an instant.

In such a ship Agent X would, very likely, get away.

Conway said, "He worked solo; his getaway was

solo. That was part of the reason he slipped through our fingers. And the ship he took was an interplanetary cruiser designed for one-man operation."

"And ships equipped with hyperspatials don't come designed for one-man operation. Not yet, anyway. But, Uncle Hector, if he's taken an interplanetary cruiser, then I suppose that's all he needs."

Lucky had finished washing and was dressing himself rapidly. He turned to Bigman suddenly. "And how about you? Snap into your clothes, Bigman."

Bigman, who was sitting on the edge of the couch, virtually turned a somersault getting off it.

Lucky said, "Probably, waiting for him somewhere in space, is a Sirian-manned ship that is equipped with hyperspatials."

"Right. And he's got a fast ship, and with his start and speed, we may not catch him or even get within weapons range. And that leaves——"

"*The Shooting Starr*. I'm ahead of you, Uncle Hector. I'll be on the *Shooter* in an hour, and Bigman with me, assuming he can drag his clothes on. Just get me the present location and course of the pursuing ships and the identifying data on Agent X's ship and we'll be on our way."

"Good." Conway's harried face smoothed out a bit. "And, David"—he used Lucky's real name, as he always did in moments of emotion—"you *will* be careful?"

"Did you ask that of the personnel on the other ten ships too, Uncle Hector?" Lucky asked, but his voice was soft and affectionate.

Bigman had one hip boot pulled up now and the other in his hand. He patted the small holster on the velvety inner surface of the free boot. "Are we on our way, Lucky?" The light of action glowed in his eyes, and his puckish little face was wrinkled in a fierce grin.

"We're on our way," said Lucky, reaching out to tousle Bigman's sandy hair. "We've been rusting on Earth for how long? Six weeks? Well, that's long enough."

"And how," agreed Bigman joyfully, and pulled on the other boot.

They were out past the orbit of Mars before they made satisfactory sub-etheric contact with the pursuing ships, using the tightest scrambling.

It was Councilman Ben Wessilewsky on the T.S.S. *Harpoon* who answered.

He shouted, "Lucky! Are you joining us? Swell!" His face grinned out of the visiplate and he winked. "Got room to squash Bigman's ugly puss into a corner of your screen? Or isn't he with you?"

"I'm with him," howled Bigman as he plunged between Lucky and the transmitter. "Think Councilman Conway would let this big lunk go anywhere without me to keep an eye on him so's he doesn't trip over his big feet?"

Lucky picked Bigman up and tucked him, squawking, under one arm. He said, "Seems to be a noisy connection, Wess. What's the position of the ship we're after?"

Wess, sobering, gave it. He said, "The ship's *The Net of Space*. It's privately owned, with a legitimate record of manufacture and sale. Agent X must have bought it under a dummy name and prepared for emergency a long time ago. It's a sweet ship and it's been accelerating ever since it took off. We're falling behind."

"What's its power capacity?"

"We've thought of that. We've checked the manufacturer's record of the craft, and at the rate he's expending power, he can't go much farther without either cutting motors or sacrificing maneuverability once he reaches destination. W're counting on driving him into that exact hole."

"Presumably, though, he may have had the sense to rev up the ship's power capacity."

"Probably," said Wess, "but even so he can't keep this up forever. The thing I worry about is the possibility that he might evade our mass detectors by asteroid-skipping. If he can get the breaks in the asteroid belt, we may lose him."

Lucky knew that trick. Place an asteroid between yourself and a pursuer, and the pursuer's mass detectors locate the asteroid rather than the ship. When a second asteroid comes within reach, the ship shifts from one to the other, leaving the pursuer with his instrument still fastened on the first rock.

Lucky said, "He's moving too fast to make the maneuver. He'd have to decelerate for half a day."

"It would take a miracle," agreed Wess frankly, "but it took a miracle to put us on his trail, and so I almost expect another miracle to cancel the first."

"What was the first miracle? The Chief said something about an emergency block."

"That's right." Wess told the story crisply, and it didn't take long. Dorrance, or Agent X (Wess called him by either name), had slipped surveillance by using an instrument that distorted the spy-beam into useless-

ness. (The instrument had been located, but its work-
ings were fused and it could not even be determined
if it was of Sirian manufacture.) He reached his getaway ship, *The Net of Space,* without trouble. He was
ready to take off with this proton micro-reactor acti-
vated, his motor and controls checked, clear space
above—and then a limping freight ship, meteor-struck
and unable to radio ahead, had appeared in the strat-
osphere, signaling desperately for a clear field.

The emergency block was flashed. All ships in port
were held fast. Any ship in the process of take-off,
unless it was already in actual motion, had to abandon
take-off procedure.

The Net of Space ought to have abandoned take-off,
but it did not. Lucky Starr could well understand
what the feelings of Agent X aboard must have been.
The hottest item in the Solar System was in his possession, and every second counted. Now that he had made
his actual move he could not rely on too long a time
before the Council would be on his heels. If he abandoned take-off it would mean an untold delay while
a riddled ship limped down and ambulances slowly
emptied it. Then, when the field was cleared again,
it would mean reactivation of the micro-reactor and
another controls check. He could not afford the delay.

So his jet blasted and up he went.

And still Agent X might have escaped. The alarm
sounded, the port police put out wild messages to *The
Net of Space,* but it was Councilman Wessilewsky,
serving a routine hitch at Port Center, who took proper
action. He had played his part in the search for
Agent X, and a ship that blasted off against an emergency block somehow smelled wildly of just enough

desperation to mean Agent X. It was the wildest possible guess, but he acted.

With the authority of the Council of Science behind him (which superseded all other authority except that contained in a direct order from the President of the Terrestrial Federation, he ordered ships into space, contacted Council Headquarters, and then boarded the T.S.S. *Harpoon* to guide the pursuit. He had already been in space for hours before the Council as a whole caught up with events. But then the message came through that he was indeed pursuing Agent X and that other ships would be joining him.

Lucky listened gravely and said, "It was a chance that paid off, Wess. And the right thing to do. Good work."

Wess grinned. Councilmen traditionally avoided publicity and the trappings of fame, but the approval of one's fellows in the Council was something greatly to be desired.

Lucky said, "I'm moving on. Have one of your ships maintain mass contact with me."

He broke visual contact, and his strong, finely formed hands closed almost caressingly on his ship's controls—his *Shooting Starr*, which in so many ways was the sweetest vessel in space.

The Shooting Starr had the most powerful proton micro-reactors that could be inserted into a ship of its size; reactors almost powerful enough to accelerate a battle cruiser at fleet-regulation pace; reactors almost powerful enough to manage the Jump through hyperspace. The ship had an ion drive that cut out most of the apparent effects of acceleration by acting simultaneously on all atoms aboard ship, including those that made up the living bodies of Lucky and Bigman. It even had an Agrav, recently developed and still experimental, which enabled it to maneuver freely in the intense gravitational fields of the major planets.

And now *The Shooting Starr's* mighty motors hummed smoothly into a higher pitch, just heard, and Lucky felt the slight pressure of such backward drag as was not completely compensated for by the ion drive. The ship bounded outward into the far reaches of the Solar System, faster, faster, still faster. . . .

And still Agent X maintained his lead, and *The Shooting Starr* gained too slowly. With the main body of the asteroid belt far behind, Lucky said, "It looks bad, Bigman."

Bigman looked surprised. "We'll get him, Lucky."

"It's where he's heading. I was sure it would be a Sirian mother-ship waiting to pick him up and make the Jump homeward. But such a ship would be either way out of the plane of the Ecliptic or it would be hidden in the asteroid belt. Either way, it could count on not being detected. But Agent X stays in the Ecliptic and heads beyond the asteroids."

"Maybe he's just trying to shake us before he heads for the ship."

"Maybe," said Lucky, "and maybe the Sirians have a base on the outer planets."

"Come on, Lucky." The small Martian cackled his derision. "Right under our noses?"

"It's hard to see under our noses sometimes. His course is aimed right at Saturn."

Bigman checked the ship's computers, which were

keeping constant tab on the other's course. He said, "Look, Lucky, the cobber is still on a ballistic course. He hasn't touched his motors in twenty million miles. Maybe he's out of power."

"And maybe he's saving his power for maneuvers in the Saturnian system. There'll be a heavy gravitational drag there. At least I *hope* he's saving power. Great Galaxy, I hope he is." Lucky's lean, handsome face was grave now and his lips were pressed together tightly.

Bigman looked at him with astonishment. "Sands of Mars, Lucky, why?"

"Because if there is a Sirian base in Saturn's system, we'll need Agent X to lead us to that base. Saturn has one tremendous satellite, eight sizeable ones, and dozens of splinter worlds. It would help to know exactly where it was."

Bigman frowned. "The cobber wouldn't be dumb enough to lead us there."

"Or maybe to let us catch him. . . . Bigman, calculate his course forward to the point of intersection with Saturn's orbit."

Bigman did so. It was a routine moment of work for the computer.

Lucky said, "And how about Saturn's position at the moment of intersection? How far will Saturn be from Agent X's ship?"

There was the short pause necessary for getting the elements of Saturn's orbit from the Ephemeris, and then Bigman punched it in. A few seconds of calculation and Bigman suddenly rose to his feet in alarm. "Lucky! Sands of Mars!"

Lucky did not need to ask the details. He said, "I'm

thinking that Agent X may have decided on the one way to keep from leading us to the Sirian base. If he continues on ballistic course exactly as he is now, he will strike Saturn itself—and sure death."

3

Death in the Rings

There came to be no possible doubt about it as the hours passed. Even the pursuing guard ships, far behind *The Shooting Starr*, too far off to get completely accurate fixes on their mass detectors, were perturbed.

Councilman Wessilewsky contacted Lucky Starr. "Space, Lucky," he said, "where's he going?"

"Saturn itself, it seems," said Lucky.

"Do you suppose a ship might be waiting for him on Saturn? I know it has thousands of miles of atmosphere with million-ton pressures, and without Agrav motors they couldn't——Lucky! Do you suppose they *have* Agrav motors and forcefield bubbles?"

"I think he may be simply crashing to keep us from catching him."

Wess said dryly, "If he's all that anxious to die, why doesn't he turn and fight, force us to destroy him and maybe take one or two of us with him?"

"I know," said Lucky, "or why not short-circuit his motors, leaving Saturn a hundred million miles off course? In fact, it bothers me that he should be attracting attention to Saturn this way." He fell into a thoughtful silence.

Wess broke in! "Well, then, can you cut him off, Lucky? Space knows *we're* too far away."

Bigman shouted from his place at the control panel, "Sands of Mars, Wess, if we rev up enough ion beam to catch him, we'll be moving too fast to maneuver him away from Saturn."

"Do *something*."

"Space, there's an intelligent order," said Bigman. "Real helpful. 'Do something'."

Lucky said, "Just keep on the move, Wess. I'll do something."

He broke contact and turned to Bigman. "Has he answered our signals at all, Bigman?"

"Not one word."

"Forget that for now and concentrate on tapping his communication beam."

"I don't think he's using one, Lucky."

"He may at the last minute. He'll have to take a chance then if he has anything to say at all. Meanwhile we're going for him."

"How?"

"Missile. Just a small pea-shot."

It was his turn to bend over the computer. While *The Net of Space* moved in an unpowered orbit, it required no great computation to direct a pellet at the proper moment and velocity to strike the fleeing ship.

Lucky readied the pellet. It was not designed to explode. It didn't have to. It was only a quarter of an inch in diameter, but the energy of the proton micropile would hurl it outward at five hundred miles a second. Nothing in space would diminish that velocity, and the pellet would pass through the hull of *The Net of Space* as though it were butter.

Lucky did not expect it would, however. The pellet would be large enough to be picked up on its quarry's mass detectors. *The Net of Space* would automatically correct course to avoid the pellet, and that would throw it off the direct course to Saturn. The time lost by Agent X in computing the new course and correcting it back to the old one might yet allow *The Shooting Starr* to come close enough to make use of a magnetic grapple.

It all added up to a slim chance, perhaps vanishingly slim, but there seemed no other possible course of action. Lucky touched a contact. The pellet sped out in a soundless flash, and the ship's mass-detector needles jumped, then quieted rapidly, as the pellet receded.

Lucky sat back. It would take two hours for the pellet to make (or almost make) contact. It occurred to him that Agent X might be completely out of power; that the automatic procedures might direct a course change which could not be followed through; that the pellet would penetrate, blow up the ship, perhaps, and in any case leave its course unchanged and still marked for Saturn.

He dismissed the idea almost at once. It would be incredible to suppose that Agent X would run out of the last bit of power at the moment his ship took on the precise collision course. It was infinitely more likely that some power was left him.

The hours of waiting were deadly. Even Hector Conway, far back on Earth, grew impatient with the periodic bulletins and made direct contact on the sub-ether.

"But where in the Saturnian system do you suppose the base might be?" he asked worriedly.

"If there is one," said Lucky cautiously, "If what Agent X is doing is not a tremendous effort to mislead us, I would say the most obvious choice is Titan. It's Saturn's one really large satellite, with three times the mass of our own Moon and over twice the surface area. If the Sirians have holed up underground, trying to dredge all of Titan for them would take a long time."

"It's hard to believe that they would have dared do this. It's virtually an act of war."

"Maybe so, Uncle Hector, but it wasn't so long ago they tried to establish a base on Ganymede."*

Bigman called out sharply, "Lucky, he's moving."

Lucky looked up in surprise. "Who's moving?"

"*The Net of Space.* The Sirian cobber."

Lucky said hastily, "I'll get in touch with you later, Uncle Hector," and broke contact. He said, "But he can't be moving, Bigman. He can't possibly have detected the pellet yet."

"Look and see for yourself, Lucky. I tell you he's moving."

Lucky, in one stride, was at the mass detectors of *The Shooting Starr.* For a long time now it had had a fix on the fleeing quarry. It had been adjusted for the ship's unpowered motion through space, and the blob that represented the detectable mass had been a small bright star mark on the screen.

But now the mark was drifting. It was a short line.

Lucky's voice was softly intense. "Great Galaxy, *of course!* Now it makes sense. How could I think his

* *Lucky Starr and the Pirates of the Asteroids.*

first duty would be merely to avoid capture? Bigman——"

"Sure, Lucky. What?" The little Martian was ready for anything.

"We're being outmaneuvered. We've got to destroy him now even if it means crashing into Saturn ourselves." For the first time since the ion-beam jets had been placed aboard *The Shooting Starr* the year before, Lucky added the emergency thrusts to the main drive. The ship reeled as every last atom of power it carried was turned into a giant thrust backward that all but burned it out.

Bigman struggled for breath. "But what's it all about, Lucky?"

"It's not Saturn he's headed for, Bigman. He was just making use of the full power of its gravitational field to help him keep ahead of us. Now he's cutting around the planet to get into orbit. It's the rings he's headed for. Saturn's rings." The young Councilman's face was drawn with tension. "Keep after that communication beam, Bigman. He'll have to talk now. Now or never."

Bigman bent over his wave analyzer with a quickening heartbeat, though for the life of him he could not understand why the thought of Saturn's rings should so disturb Lucky.

The Shooting Starr's pellet came nowhere near its mark, not within fifty thousand miles. But now it was *The Shooting Starr* itself that was a pellet, striving for junction; and it, too, would miss.

Lucky groaned. "We'll never make it. There's not enough room left to make it."

Saturn was a giant in the sky now, with its rings a

thin gash across its face. Saturn's yellow globe was almost at the full as *The Shooting Starr* burned toward it from the direction of the Sun.

And Bigman suddenly exploded, "Why, the dirty cobber! He's melting into the rings, Lucky. Now I see what got you about the rings."

He worked furiously at the mass detector, but it was hopeless. As a portion of the rings came into focus, each of the countless solid masses that composed them formed its own star mark on the screen. The screen turned pure white and *The Net of Space* was gone.

Lucky shook his head. "That's not an insoluble problem. We're close enough to get a visual fix now. It's something else that I'm sure is coming."

Lucky, pale and engrossed, had the visiplate under maximum telescopic enlargement. *The Net of Space* was a tiny metal cylinder obscured but not hidden by the material of the rings. The individual particles in the rings were no larger than coarse gravel and were only sparkles as they caught and threw back the light of the distant Sun.

Bigman said, "Lucky! I've got his communications beam. . . . No, no, wait now. . . . Yes, I have it."

There was a wavering voice crackling in the control room now, obscured and distorted. Bigman's deft fingers worked at the unscrambler, trying to fit it better and ever better with the unknown characteristics of the Sirian scrambling system.

The words would die out, then come back. There was silence except for the faint hum of the recorder taking down permanently whatever came through.

". . . not . . . wor . . . hither . . ." (Quite a pause while Bigman fought frantically with his detectors.)

". . . on trail and . . . couldn't shake . . . done for and I must transmit . . . rn's rings in normal orb . . . dy launch . . . stics of or . . . follow . . . co-ordinate read thus . . ."

It broke off altogether at that precise point; the voice, the static, everything.

Bigman yelled, "Sands of Mars, something's blown!"

"Nothing here," said Lucky. "It's *The Net of Space*."

He had seen it happen two seconds after transmission ceased. Transmission through the sub-ether was at virtually infinite velocity. The light that he saw through the visiplate traveled at only 186,000 miles a second.

It took two seconds for the sight of it to reach Lucky. He saw the rear end of *The Net of Space* glow a cherry-red, then open and spatter into a flower of melting metal.

Bigman caught the tail end of it, and he and Lucky watched wordlessly until radiation cooled the spectacle.

Lucky shook his head. "That close to the rings, even though you're outside the main body of them, space has more than its share of speeding material. Maybe he had no further power to run the ship out of the way of one of those bits. Or maybe two pieces converged at him from slightly different directions. In any case, he was a brave man and clever enemy."

"I don't get it, Lucky. What was he doing?"

"Don't you see even now? While it was important for him not to fall into our hands, it wasn't enough for him to die. I should have seen that earlier myself. His most important task was to get the stolen information in his possession to Sirius. He didn't dare risk the

sub-ether for reeling off what may have been thousands
of words of information—with ships in pursuit and
possibly tapping his beam. He had to restrict his message to the briefest essentials and see to it that the
capsule was placed bodily in the grip of the Sirians."

'   "How could he do that?"

"What we caught of his message contains the syllable "orb"—probably for "orbit"—and "dy launch,"
meaning "already launched.""

Bigman caught at Lucky's arms, his small fingers
pinching tightly on the other's sinewy wrists. "He
launched the capsule into the rings; is that it, Lucky?
It'll be a piece of gravel along with a zillion other
pieces, like—a pebble on the Moon—or a water drop
in an ocean."

"Or," said Lucky, "like a piece of gravel in Saturn's
rings, which is worst of all. Of course he was destroyed
before he could give the co-ordinates of the orbit he
had chosen for the capsule, so the Sirians and we
start even, and we had better make the most of that
without delay."

"Start looking? Now?"

"Now! If he was ready to give the co-ordinates,
knowing I was hot after him, he must also have known
the Sirians were close by. . . . Contact the ships, Bigman, and give them the news."

Bigman turned to the transmitter but never touched
it. The reception button was glowing with intercepted
radio waves. Radio! Ordinary etheric communication!
Obviously someone was close by (certainly within
the Saturnian system), and someone, moreover, felt
not the least desire for secrecy, since a radio beam, un-

like sub-etheric communication, was childishly simple to tap.

Lucky's eyes narrowed. "Let's receive, Bigman."

The voice came through with that trace of accent, that broadening of vowels and sharpening of consonants. It was a Sirian voice.

It said, "—fy yourselves before we are forced to place a grapple on you and take you into custody. You have fourteen minutes to acknowledge reception." There was a minute's pause. "By authority of the Central Body, you are ordered to identify yourself before we are forced to place a grapple on you and take you into custody. You have thirteen minutes to acknowledge reception."

Lucky said coldly, "Reception acknowledged. This is *The Shooting Starr* of the Terrestrial Federation, orbiting peacefully in the spatial volume of the Terrestrial Federation. No authority other than that of the Federation exists in these spaces."

There was a second or two of silence (radio waves travel with only the speed of light) and the voice retorted, "The authority of the Terrestrial Federation is not recognized on a world colonized by the Sirian peoples."

"Which world is that?" asked Lucky.

"The uninhabited Saturnian system has been taken possession of in the name of our government under the interstellar law that awards any uninhabited world to those who colonize it."

"Not any uninhabited world. Any uninhabited stellar system."

There was no answer. The voice said stolidly,

"You are now within the Saturnian system and you are requested to leave forthwith. Any delay in acceleration outward will result in our taking you into custody. Any further ships of the Terrestrial Federation entering our territory will be taken into custody without additional warning. Your acceleration out of the Saturnian system must begin within eight minutes or we will take action."

Bigman, his face twisted with unholy glee, whispered, "Let's go in and get them, Lucky. Let's show them the old *Shooter* can fight."

But Lucky paid no attention. He said into the transmitter, "Your remark is noted. We do not accept Sirian authority, but we choose, of our own will, to leave and will now do so." He snapped off contact.

Bigman was appalled. "Sands of Mars, Lucky! Are we going to run from a bunch of *Sirians?* Are we going to leave that capsule in Saturn's rings for the Sirians to pick up?"

Lucky said, "Right now, Bigman, we have to." His head was bent and his face was pale and strained, but there was something in his eyes that was not quite that of a man backing down. Anything but that.

4

Between Jupiter and Saturn

The ranking officer in the pursuing squadron (not counting Councilman Wessilewsky, of course) was Captain Myron Bernold. He was a four-striper, still under fifty, and with the physique of a man ten years younger. His hair was graying, but his eyebrows were still their original black and his beard showed blue about his shaven chin.

He stared at the much younger Lucky Starr with undisguised scorn. *"And you backed away?"*

The Shooting Starr, having headed inward toward the Sun again, had met the ships of the squadron approximately halfway between the orbits of Jupiter and Saturn. Lucky had boarded the flagship.

He said now quietly, "I did what was necessary to be done."

"When the enemy had invaded our home system, retreat can never be necessary. You might have been blown out of space, but you would have had time to warn us and we would have been there to take over."

"With how much power left in your micro-pile units, Captain?"

The captain flushed. "Nor would it matter if we

got blasted out of space. That couldn't have been done before we had, in our turn, alerted home base."

"And started a war?"

"*They*'ve started the war. The Sirians. . . . It is now my intention to move on to Saturn and attack."

Lucky's own rangy figure stiffened. He was taller than the captain, and his cool glance did not waver. "As full Councilman of the Council of Science, Captain, I outrank you and you know it. I will give no orders to attack. The orders I give you are to return to Earth."

"I would sooner——" The captain was visibly struggling with his temper. His fists clenched. He said in a strangled voice, "May I ask the reason for the order, sir?" He emphasized the syllable of respect with heavy irony. "If, sir, you would be so good as to explain the excellent reason you no doubt have, sir. My own reasoning is based on a small tradition that the fleet happens to have. A tradition, sir, that the fleet does not retreat, sir."

Lucky said, "If you want my reasons, Captain, sit down and I'll give them to you. And don't tell me the fleet does not retreat. Retreat is a part of the maneuver of war, and a commanding officer who would rather have his ships destroyed than retreat has no business in command. I think it's only your anger that's speaking. Now, Captain, are we ready to start a war?"

"I tell you they have already started. They have invaded the Terrestrial Federation."

"Not exactly. They've occupied an unoccupied world. The trouble is, Captain, that the Jump through hyperspace has made travel to the stars so simple that

Earthmen have colonized the planets of other stars long before ever colonizing the remoter portions of our own Solar System."

"Terrestrials have landed on Titan. In the year——"

"I know about the flight of James Francis Hogg. He landed on Oberon in the Uranian system also. But that was just exploration, not colonization. The Saturnian system was left empty, and an unoccupied world belongs to the first group that colonizes it."

"If," said the captain heavily, "that unoccupied planet or planetary system is part of an unoccupied stellar system. Saturn isn't that, you'll admit. It's part of our Solar System, which, by the howling devils of space, is occupied."

"True, but I don't think there is any official agreement to that effect. Perhaps it may be decided that Sirius is within its rights in occupying Saturn."

The captain brought his fist down upon his knee. "I don't care what the space lawyers say. Saturn is ours, and any Earthman with blood in him will agree. We'll kick the Sirians off and let our weapons decide the law."

"But that's exactly what Sirius would want us to do!"

"Then let's give her what she wants."

"And we will be accused of aggression. . . . Captain, there are fifty worlds out there among the stars who never forget that they were our colonies once. We gave them their freedom without a war, but they forget that. They only remember we are still the most populous and most advanced of all the worlds. If Sirius shouts we have committed unprovoked aggression, she'll unite them against us. It is just for that reason that she is trying to provoke us to attack now, and it is just for that reason that I refused the invitation and came away."

The captain bit at his lower lip and would have answered, but Lucky drove on.

"On the other hand, if we do nothing, we can accuse the Sirians of aggression and we'll split public opinion in the outer worlds wide open. We can exploit that and bring them to our own side."

"The outer worlds to *our* side?"

"Why not? There isn't a stellar system in existence that doesn't have hundreds of unoccupied worlds of all sizes. They won't want to set up a precedent that would set every system to raiding every other system for bases. The only danger is that we will stampede them into opposition to us by making it look as if we are powerful Earth throwing our weight about against our former colonies."

The captain rose from his seat and strode the length of his quarters and then back. He said, "Repeat your orders."

Lucky said, "Do you understand my reason for retreat?"

"Yes. May I have my orders?"

"Very well. I order you to deliver this Capsule I now give you to Chief Councilman Hector Conway. You are not to discuss anything that has happened during this pursuit with anyone else, either on the sub-ether or in any other fashion. You are to take no hostile action—repeat, no hostile action—against any Sirian forces, unless directly attacked. And if you go out of your way to meet such forces, or if you deliberately provoke attack, I shall see you court-martialed and convicted. Is all clear?"

The captain stood frozen-faced. His lips moved as though they were carved out of wood and badly hinged. "With all due respect, sir, would it be possible for the Councilman to take over command of my ships and deliver the message himself?"

Lucky Starr shrugged slightly and said, "You are very obstinate, Captain, and I even admire you for it. There are times in battle when this kind of bull-doggedness can be useful. . . . It is impossible for me to deliver this message, since it is my intention to return to *The Shooting Starr* and blast off for Saturn again."

The captain's military rigidity came unstuck. "What? Howling space, *what?*"

"I thought my statement was plain, Captain. I have left something undone there. My first task was to see to it that Earth was warned of the terrible political danger we are facing. If you will take care of that warning for me, I can carry on where I now belong—back in the Saturnian system."

The captain was grinning broadly. "Well, now, that's different. I would like to come along with you."

"I know that, Captain. Sheering away from a fight is the harder task for you, and I'm asking you to do it because I expect you are used to hard tasks. Now I want each of your ships to transfer some of their power into the micro-pile units of *The Shooting Starr*. There'll be other supplies I'll need from your stores."

"You need only ask."

"Very good. I will return to my ship and I will ask Councilman Wessilewsky to join me in my mission."

He shook hands briefly with the now thoroughly friendly captain, and then Councilman Wessilewsky joined him as Lucky stepped into the inter-ship tube that snaked between the flagship and *The Shooting Starr*.

The inter-ship tube was at nearly its full extension, and it took several minutes to negotiate its length. The tube was airless, but the two Councilmen could maintain space-suit contact easily and sound waves would travel along the metal to emerge squawkily but distinctly enough. And, after all, no form of communication is quite as private as sound waves over short range, so it was in the air tube that Lucky was able to speak briefly to the other.

Finally Wess, changing the subject slightly, said, "Listen, Lucky, if the Sirians are trying to start trouble, why did they let you go? Why not have harassed you till you were forced to turn and fight?"

"As for that, Wess, you listen to the recording of what the Sirian ship had to say. There was a stiffness about the words; a failure to threaten actual harm, only magnetic grappling. I'm convinced it was a robot-piloted ship."

"Robots!" Wess's eyes widened.

"Yes. Judge from your own reaction what Earth's would be if that speculation got about. The fact is that those robot-piloted ships could have done no harm to a human-piloted ship. The First Law of Robotics—that no robot can harm a human—would have prevented it. And that just made the danger greater. If I had attacked, as they probably expected me to, the Sirians would have insisted that I had made a murderous and unprovoked assault on defenseless vessels. And the outer worlds appreciate the facts of robotics as Earth does not. No, Wess, the only way I could cross them was to leave, and I did."

With that, they were at the air-lock of *The Shooting Starr*.

Bigman was waiting for them. There was the usual grin of relief on his face at meeting Lucky again after even the smallest separation.

"Hey," he said. "What do you know? You didn't fall out of the inter-ship tube after all and——What's Wess doing here?"

"He's coming with us, Bigman."

The little Martian looked annoyed. "What for? This is a two-man ship we've got here."

"We'll manage a guest temporarily. And now we'd better get set to drain power from the other ships and receive equipment along the tube. After that we make ready for instant blast-off."

Lucky's voice was firm, his change of subject definite. Bigman knew better than to argue.

He muttered, "Sure thing," and stepped across into the engine room after one malignant scowl in the direction of Councilman Wessilewsky.

Wess said, "Now what's eating him? I haven't said a word about his size."

Lucky said, "Well, you have to understand the little fellow. He's not a Councilman officially, although he is one for all practical purposes. He's the only one who doesn't realize that. Anyway, he thinks that because you're another Councilman we'll get chummy and cut him out; have our little secrets from him."

Wess nodded. "I see. Are you suggesting then that we tell him——"

"No." The stress on the word was soft, but emphatic. "I'll tell him what has to be told. You say nothing."

At that moment Bigman stepped into the pilot room again and said, "She's sopping up the power," then looked from one to the other and growled, "Well, sorry I'm interrupting. Shall I leave the ship, gentlemen?"

Lucky said, "You'll have to knock me down first, Bigman."

Bigman made rapid sparring motions and said, "Oh boy, what a difficult task. You think an extra foot of clumped fat makes it any job?"

With blinding speed he was inside Lucky's arm as it was thrown out laughingly toward him, and his fists landed one-two, thwackingly, in Lucky's midsection.

Lucky said, "Feel better?"

Bigman danced back. "I pulled my punch because I didn't want Councilman Conway bawling me out for hurting you."

Lucky laughed. "Thank you. Now listen, I've got an orbit for you to calculate and send on to Captain Bernold."

"Sure thing." Bigman seemed quite at ease now, any rancor gone.

Wess said, "Listen, Lucky, I hate to act the wet blanket, but we're not very far from Saturn. It seems to me that the Sirians will have a fix on us right now and know exactly where we are, when we leave, and where we go."

"I think so too, Wess."

"Well, then, how in space do we leave the squadron and head back for Saturn without their knowing exactly where we are and heading us off too far from the system for our purposes?"

"Good question. I was wondering if you'd guess how. If you didn't, I was reasonably certain the Sirians wouldn't guess either, and they don't know the details of our system nearly as well as we do."

Wess leaned back in his pilot's chair. "Let's not make a mystery of it, Lucky."

"It's perfectly plain. All the ships, including ourselves, blast-off in tight formation, so that, considering the distance between the Sirians and ourselves, we'll register as a single spot on their mass detectors. We maintain that formation, flying on almost the minimum orbit to Earth, but just enough off course to make a reasonable approach to the asteroid Hidalgo, which is now moving out toward aphelion."

"Hidalgo?"

"Come on, Wess, you know it. It's a perfectly legitimate asteroid and known since the primeval days before space travel. The interesting thing about it is that it doesn't stay in the asteroid belt. At its closest to the Sun it moves in as close as the orbit of Mars, but at its farthest it moves out almost as far as Saturn's orbit. Now when we pass near it, Hidalgo will register on the Sirian mass-detection screens also, and from the strength with which it will register they'll know it to be an asteroid. Then they'll spot the mass of our ships moving on past Hidalgo toward Earth and they won't spot the less than ten per cent total decrease in ship's mass that will result when *The Shooting Starr* turns and heads back out from the Sun in Hidalgo's shadow. Hidalgo's path isn't directly toward the present position of Saturn by any means, but after two days in its shadow we can head well out of Ecliptic toward Saturn and rely on not being detected."

Wess raised his eyebrows. "I hope it works, Lucky."

He saw the strategy. The plane in which all the planets and commercial space-flight routes lay was the Ecliptic. One practically never looked for anything moving well above or below that zone. It was reasonable to suppose that a space ship moving on the orbit being planned by Lucky would evade Sirian instruments. Yet there was still the look of uncertainty on Wess's face.

Lucky said, "Do you think we'll make it?"

Wess said, "Maybe we will. But even if we do get back—— Lucky, I'm in this and I'll do my part, but just let me say this once and I'll never say it again. I think we're as good as dead!"

5

Skimming Saturn's Surface

And so *The Shooting Starr* flashed alongside Hidalgo and then out on the flight beyond the Ecliptic and up again toward the southern polar regions of the Solar System's second largest planet.

At no time in their still short history of space adventure had Lucky and Bigman remained in space for so long a period without a break. It had been nearly a month now since they had left Earth. However, the small bubble of air and warmth that was *The Shooting Starr* was a bit of Earth that could keep itself so for an almost indefinite period to come.

Their power supply, built to maximum by the donation of the other ships, would last nearly a year, barring a full-scale battle. Their air and water, recirculated by way of the algae tanks, would last a lifetime. The algae even provided a food reserve in case their more orthodox concentrates ran out.

It was the presence of the third man that made for the only real discomfort. As Bigman had pointed out, *The Shooting Starr* was built for two. Its unusual concentration of power, speed, and armaments was made possible partly by the unusual economy of its living quarters. So turns had to be taken in sleeping on a quilt in the pilot room.

Lucky pointed out that any discomfort was made up for by the fact that four-hour watches at the controls could now be set up rather than the usual six-hour watches.

To which Bigman replied hotly, "Sure, and when I'm trying to sleep on this doggone blanket and Fat-face Wess is at the controls, he keeps flashing every signal light right in my face."

"Twice each watch," said Wess patiently, "I check the various emergency signals to make sure they're in order. That's protocol."

"And," said Bigman, "he keeps whistling through his teeth. Listen, Lucky, if he gives me one more chorus of 'My Sweet Aphrodite of Venus'—just once more—I'll up and break off his arms halfway between shoulder and elbow, then beat him to death with the stumps."

Lucky said gravely, "Wess, please refrain from whistling refrains. If Bigman is forced to chastise you, he will get blood all over the pilot room."

Bigman said nothing, but the next time he was at the controls, with Wess asleep on the blanket and snoring musically, he managed somehow to step on the fingers of Wess's outstretched hand as he made for the pilot's stool.

"Sands of Mars," he said, holding up both hands, palms forward, and rolling his eyes at the other's sudden, tigerish yell. "I did think I felt something under my heavy Martian boots. My, my, Wess, was it your little thumbikins?"

"You better stay awake from now on," yelled Wess

in furious agony. "Because if you go to sleep while I'm in the control room, you Martian sand rat, I'll squash you like a bug."

"I'm so frightened," said Bigman, going into a paroxysm of mock weeping that brought Lucky wearily out of his bunk.

"Listen," he said, "the next one of you two who wakes me trails the *Shooter* in his suit at the end of a cable for the rest of the trip."

But when Saturn and its rings came into near view, they were all in the pilot room, watching. Even as seen in the usual manner, from an equatorial view, Saturn was the most beautiful sight in the Solar System, and from a polar view. . .

"If I recall correctly," said Lucky, "even Hogg's exploratory voyage touched this system only at Japetus and Titan, so that he saw only an equatorial view of Saturn. Unless the Sirians have done differently, we're the first human beings ever to see Saturn this close from this direction."

As with Jupiter, the soft yellow glow of Saturn's "surface" was really the reflected sunlight from the upper layers of a turbulent atmosphere a thousand miles or more in depth. And, as with Jupiter, the atmospheric disturbances showed up as zones of varying colors. But the zones were not the stripes they appeared to be from the usual equatorial view. Instead, they formed concentric circles of soft brown, lighter yellow, and pastel green about the Saturnian pole as a center.

But even that faded to nothing compared to the rings. At their present distance, the rings stretched

over an arc of twenty-five degrees, fifty times the width
of Earth's full Moon. The inner edge of the rings was
separated from the planet by a space of forty-five minutes of arc in which there was room to hold an object
the size of the full Moon loosely enough to allow it to
rattle.

The rings circled Saturn, touching it nowhere from
the viewpoint of *The Shooting Starr*. They were visible
for about three fifths of their circle, the rest being cut
off sharply by Saturn's shadow. About three fourths
of the way toward the outer edge of the ring was the
black separation known as "Cassini's division." It was
about fifteen minutes wide, a thick ribbon of black-
ness, dividing the rings into two paths of brightness of
unequal width. Within the inner lip of the rings was a
scattering of sparkle that shimmered but did not form
a continuous whiteness. This was the so-called "crepe
ring."

The total area exposed by the rings was more than
eight times as great as that of the globe of Saturn.
Furthermore, the rings themselves were obviously
brighter, area for area, than Saturn itself, so that on the
whole at least ninety per cent of the light reaching them
from the planet came from its rings. The total light
reaching them was about one hundred times that of
Earth's full Moon.

Even Jupiter as seen from that startling nearness of
Io was somehow nothing like this. When Bigman finally spoke, it was in a whisper.

He said, "Lucky, how come the rings are so bright?
It makes Saturn itself look dim. Is that an optical
illusion?"

"No," said Lucky, "it's real. Both Saturn and the

rings get the same amount of light from the Sun, but they don't reflect the same amount. What we're seeing from Saturn is the light reflected from an atmosphere made up of hydrogen and helium, mainly, plus some methane. That reflects about sixty-three per cent of the light that hits it. The rings, however, are mostly solid chunks of ice, and they send back a minimum of eighty per cent, which makes them that much brighter. Looking at the rings is like looking at a field of snow."

Wess mourned, "And we've got to find one snow-flake in the field of snow.

"But a *dark* snowflake," said Bigman excitedly. "Listen, Lucky, if all the ring particles are ice and we're looking for a capsule that's metal——"

"Polished aluminum," said Lucky, "will reflect even more light than will ice. It will be just as shiny."

"Well, then"——Bigman looked despairingly at the rings half a million miles away, yet so tremendous in area even at that distance— "this thing is hopeless."

"We'll see," said Lucky noncommittally.

Bigman sat at the controls, adjusting orbit in short, quiet bursts of the ion drive. The Agrav controls had been connected so that *The Shooting Starr* was far more maneuverable in this volume of space, so close to the mass of Saturn, than any Sirian ship could possibly be.

Lucky was at the mass detector, the delicate probe of which scoured space for any matter, fixing its position by measuring its response to the gravitational force of the ship, if it were small, or the effect of its gravitational force upon the ship, if it were large.

Wess had just awakened and entered the pilot room,

and all was silence and tension as the ship sank toward
Saturn. Bigman watched Lucky's face out of the corner of his eye. Lucky had grown more and more
abstracted as Saturn came near, abstracted and un-
communicative. Bigman had witnessed this before.
Lucky was uncertain; he was gambling on poor odds
and he would not talk of it.

Wess said, "I don't think you have to be sweating
over the mass detector so, Lucky. There'll be no ships
up here. It's when we get down to the rings that we'll
find the ships. Plenty of them, probably. The Sirians
will be looking for the capsule too."

"I agree with that," said Lucky, "as far as it goes."

"Maybe," said Bigman gloomily, "those cobbers
have found the capsule already."

"Even that's possible," admitted Lucky.

They were turning now, beginning to edge along the
circle of Saturn's globe, maintaining an eight-thou-
sand-mile distance from its surface. The far half of
the rings (or at least the portion that was in the sunlight) melted into Saturn as its inner edge was hidden
by the giant planetary bulge.

In the case of the half rings on the near side of the
planet, the inner "crepe ring" became more noticeable.

Bigman said, "You know, I don't make out any
end to that inside ring."

Wess said, "There isn't any end, probably. The innermost part of the main rings is only six thousand
miles above Saturn's apparent surface, and Saturn's
atmosphere may stretch out that far."

"Six thousand miles!"

"Just in wisps, but enough to supply friction for
the nearest bits of gravel and make them circle a bit
closer to Saturn. Those that move in closer form the

crepe ring. Only the closer they move, the more friction there is, so that they must move still closer. There are probably particles all the way down to Saturn, with some burning up as they hit the thicker layer of the atmosphere."

Bigman said, "Then the rings aren't going to last forever."

"Probably not. But they'll last millions of years. Long enough for us." He added somberly, "Too long."

Lucky interrupted, "I'm leaving the ship, gentlemen."

"Sands of Mars, Lucky. What for?" Bigman cried.

"I want an outside look," Lucky answered curtly. He was pulling on his space suit.

Bigman glanced quickly at the automatic record of the mass detector. No ships in space. There were occasional jogs, but nothing important. They were only the kind of drifting meteorites that were picked up anywhere in the Solar System.

Lucky said, "Take over at the mass detector, Wess. Let it take a round-the-clock sweep." Lucky put his helmet on and clicked it into place. He checked the gauges on his chest, the oxygen pressure, and moved toward the air lock. His voice now emerged from the small radio receiver on the control board. "I'll be using a magnetic cable, so make no sudden power thrusts."

"With you out there? Think I'm crazy?" said Bigman.

Lucky came into view at one of the ports, the magnetic cable snaking behind him in coils that, in the absence of gravity, did not form a smooth curve.

A small hand reactor in his gauntleted fist shot out its small jet stream, which became faintly visible in the weak sunlight as a cloud of tiny ice particles that dispersed and vanished. Lucky, by the law of action and reaction, moved in the opposite direction.

Bigman said, "Do you suppose something's wrong with the ship?"

"If there is," said Wess, "it doesn't show up anywhere on the control board."

"Then what's the big lug doing?"

"I don't know."

But Bigman shot a suspicious glare at the Councilman, then turned again to watch Lucky. "If you think," he muttered, "because I'm not a Councilman——"

Wess said, "Maybe he just wanted to get outside range of your voice for a few minutes, Bigman."

The mass detector, on automatic sweep control, was moving methodically across the volume about them, square degree by square degree, the screen blanking out into pure white whenever it edged too far in the direction of Saturn itself.

Bigman scowled and lacked heart to respond to Wess's thrust. "I wish something would happen," he said.

And something did.

Wess, eyes returning to the mass detector, caught a suspicious pip on the recorder. He fixed the instrument on it hurriedly, brought up the auxiliary energy detectors, and followed it for two minutes.

Bigman said excitedly, "It's a ship, Wess."

"Looks like it," said Wess reluctantly. Mass alone might have meant a large meteorite, but there was a blast of energy being emitted from that direction that could come only from the micro-pile engines of a ship; the energy was of the right type and in the right quantities. It was as identifiable as a fingerprint. One could even detect the slight differences from the energy pattern produced by Terrestrial ships and identify this object unmistakably as a Sirian ship.

Bigman said, "It's heading for us."

"Not directly. Probably it doesn't dare take chances with Saturn's gravitational field. Still it's edging closer, and in about an hour it will be in position to lay down a barrage against us. . . .What in space are you so pleased about, you Martian farm boy?"

"Isn't it obvious, you lump of fat? This explains why Lucky's out there. He knew the ship was coming and he's laying a trap for it."

"How in space could he tell a ship was coming?" demanded Wess in astonishment. "There was no indication on the mass detector till ten minutes ago. It wasn't even focused in the proper direction."

"Don't worry about Lucky. He has a way of knowing." Bigman was grinning.

Wess shrugged, moved to the control panel, and called into the transmitter, "Lucky! Do you hear me?"

"Sure I hear you, Wess. What's up?"

"There's a Sirian ship in mass-detection range."

"How close?"

"Under two hundred thousand and getting closer."

Bigman, watching out the port, noticed the flash of Lucky's hand reactor, and ice crystals swirled away from the ship. Lucky was returning.

"I'm coming in," he said.

Bigman spoke at once, as soon as the helmet was lifted off Lucky's head to reveal his brown shock of hair and his clear brown eyes. Bigman said, "You knew that ship was coming, didn't you, Lucky?"

"No, Bigman. I had no idea. In fact, I don't understand how they discovered us so quickly. It's asking too much of coincidence to suppose they just happened to be looking in this direction."

Bigman tried to mask his chagrin. "Well, then, do we blast him out of space, Lucky?"

"Let's not go through the political dangers of attack again, Bigman. Besides, we have a mission here that's more important than playing shooting games with other ships."

"I know," said Bigman impatiently. "There's the capsule we've got to find, but——"

He shook his head. A capsule was a capsule and he understood its importance. But then, a good fight was a good fight, and Lucky's political reasoning about the dangers of aggression did not appeal to him if it meant ducking a fight. He muttered, "What do I do then? Stay on course?"

"And accelerate. Make for the rings."

"If we do," said Bigman, "they'll just take out after us."

"All right. We'll race."

Bigman drew back the control rod slowly, and the proton disintegrations in the micro-pile increased to top fury. The ship hurtled along the bulging curve of Saturn.

At once the reception disk was alive with the impingement of radio waves.

"Shall we go into active reception, Lucky?" asked Wess.

"No, we know what they'll say. Surrender or be magnetically grappled."

"Well?"

"Our only chance is to run."

6

Through the Gap

"From one rotten ship, Lucky?" wailed Bigman.

"Time enough to fight later, Bigman. First things first."

"But it just means we've got to leave Saturn again."

Lucky smiled humorlessly. "Not this time, Bigman. This time we establish a base in this planet's system—and just as fast as we can."

The ship was hurtling toward the rings at blinding velocity. Lucky nudged Bigman away from the controls and took over.

Wess said, "More ships showing."

"Where? What satellite are they nearest to?"

Wess worked quickly. "They're all in the ring region."

"Well," muttered Lucky, "then they're still hunting for the capsule. How many ships are there?"

"Five so far, Lucky."

"Any between us and the rings?"

"A sixth ship has shown. We aren't being stymied, Lucky. They're all too far to shoot with any accuracy, but they're going to track us down eventually unless we leave the Saturnian system altogether."

"Or unless our ship is destroyed in some other fashion, eh?" said Lucky grimly.

The rings had expanded in size till they filled the visiplate with snowy white, and still the ship careened onward. Nor did Lucky make any move to decelerate.

For one horrified moment Bigman thought Lucky was going to crash the ship among the rings deliberately. He let out an involuntary "Lucky!"

And then the rings disappeared.

Bigman was dazed. His hands went to the visiplate controls. He cried, "Where are they? What happened?"

Wess, sweating it out over the mass detectors and rumpling his yellow hair with occasional restless yanks, called over his shoulder, "Cassini division."

"What?"

"The division between the rings."

"Oh." Some of the shock was wearing off. Bigman swiveled the visiplate eyepiece on the ship's hull, and the snowy whiteness of the rings flashed back into view. He maneuvered it more carefully.

First there was one ring. Then space, black space. Then another ring, somewhat dimmer. The outer ring was a trifle less thickly strewn with icy gravel. Back to the space between the rings. Cassini's division. No gravel there. Just a wide black gap.

"It's big," said Bigman.

Wess wiped the perspiration from his forehead and looked at Lucky. "Are we going through, Lucky?"

Lucky kept his eyes fixed on the controls. "We're going through, Wess, in a matter of minutes. Hold your breath and hope."

Wess turned on Bigman and said curtly, "Sure the

division is big. I told you it was twenty-five hundred miles wide. Plenty of room for the ship, if that's what's scaring you."

Bigman said, "You sound kind of nervous yourself for a fellow six feet tall on the outside. Is Lucky moving too fast for you?"

Wess said, "Look, Bigman, if I took it into my head to sit down on you——"

"Then there'd be more brains where you're sitting on than in your head," and Bigman burst out into a delighted squawk of laughter.

Lucky said, "In five minutes we'll be in the division."

Bigman choked off and turned back to the visiplate. He said, "There's a kind of twinkle every once in a while inside the gap."

Lucky said, "That's gravel, Bigman. The Cassini division is clear of it, compared with the rings themselves, but they're not a hundred per cent clear. If we hit one of those bits on the way through——"

"One chance in a thousand," broke in Wess, shrugging it off.

"One chance in a million," said Lucky coolly, "but it was that one chance in a million that got Agent X in *The Net of Space*. . . . We're about at the boundary of the division proper." His hand held firmly at the controls.

Bigman drew a deep breath, tensing for the possible puncture that would rip the hull and perhaps short the proton micro-pile into a spreading blaze of red energy. At least it would be over before. . .

Lucky said, "Made it."

Wess let out his breath noisily.

Bigman said, "Are we through?"

"Of course we're through, you dumb Martian," said Wess. "The rings are only ten miles thick, and how many seconds do you think it takes us to make ten miles?"

"And we're on the other side?"

"You bet. Try to find the rings on the visiplate."

Bigman veered the view one way, then back in the other direction, then over and over again in continuously longer sweeps. "Sands of Mars, there's a kind of shadowy outline there."

"And that's all you'll see, little pal. You're on the shadow side of the rings now. The Sun's lighting up the other side, and the light doesn't seep through ten miles of thick gravel. Say, Bigman, what do they teach for astronomy in the Martian schools, anyway—'Twinkle, twinkle, little star'?"

Bigman's lower lip thrust out slowly. "You know, lardhead, I'd like to have you one season on the Martian farms. I'd render some of the fat off you and get down to what meat you have, about ten pounds of it—and all of it in your big feet."

Lucky said, "I'd appreciate it, Wess, if you and Bigman would put a bookmark in that argument you're having and save it for later. Would you check on the mass detector, please?"

"Sure thing, Lucky. Hey, it's way off kilter. How sharply are you changing course?"

"As sharply as the ship will take. We're staying under the rings all the distance we can."

Wess nodded. "Okay, Lucky. That knocks out their mass detection."

Bigman grinned. It worked out perfectly. No mass

detector could spot *The Shooting Starr* because of the interference of the mass of Saturn's rings, and even visual detection was unlikely through the rings.

Lucky's long legs stretched out, and the muscles of his back moved smoothly as he stretched and flexed some of the tension out of his arms and shoulders.

"I doubt," said Lucky, "that any of the Sirian ships will have the nerve to follow us through the gap. They don't have Agrav."

"Okay," said Bigman, "so far, so good. But where do we go now? Will anyone tell me?"

"No secret," said Lucky. "We're heading for Mimas. We hug the rings till we're as close to Mimas as we can get, then make the dash across the intervening space. Mimas is only thirty thousand miles outside the rings."

"Mimas? That's one of the moons of Saturn, right?"

"Right," said Wess, breaking in. "The nearest one to the planet."

Their course had flattened out now, and *The Shooting Starr* was still moving around Saturn, but west to east now, in a plane parallel with the rings.

Wess sat down on the blanket, legs crossed under him like a tailor, and said, "Would you like to learn a little more astronomy? If you can find a little room in that walnut you have in your hollow skull, I can tell you why there's a division in the rings."

Curiosity and scorn battled in the small Martian. He said, "Let's see you make up something fast, you ignorant cobber. Go ahead, I call your bluff."

"No bluff," said Wess haughtily. "Listen and learn. The inner parts of the two rings rotate about Saturn in five hours. The outermost parts make the rotation in fifteen hours. Right where Cassini's division is, the ring material, if there were any there, would go around at an intermediate rate, twelve hours per circuit."

"So what?"

"So the satellite Mimas, the one we're heading for, travels around Saturn in twenty-four hours."

"Again, so what?"

"All the particles in the ring are pulled this way and that by the satellites as they and the satellites move about Saturn. Mimas does most of the pulling because it is the closest. Mostly the pulls are in one direction now and in another direction an hour from now, so that they cancel out. If there were gravel in Cassini's division, however, every second time it completed its rotation it would find Mimas in the same spot in the sky, pulling in the same old direction. Some of the gravel is constantly pulled ahead, so that it spirals outward into the outer ring; and some of it is pulled back, so that it spirals inward into the inner ring. They don't stay where they are; a section of the ring empties of particles and bingo—you have Cassini's division and two rings."

"Is that so?" said Bigman weakly (he felt reasonably certain Wess was giving him the correct story). "Then how come there *is* some gravel in the division? Why isn't it all moved out by now?"

"Because," said Wess with a lofty air of superiority, "some is always being pushed in or pulled in by random gravitational effects of the satellites, but none of it ever stays long. . . . And I hope you're taking notes on all this, Bigman, because I may ask questions on this later."

"Go fry your skull in a mesonic blast," muttered Bigman.

Wess returned to his mass detectors again, smiling. He fiddled with them a moment, then with no trace of the preceding banter left on his leathery face, he bent down closely.

"Lucky!"

"Yes, Wess?"

"The rings aren't masking us."

"What?"

"Well, look for yourself. The Sirians are getting closer. The rings aren't bothering them at all."

Lucky said thoughtfully, "Why, how can that be?"

"It can't be blind luck that's converging eight ships on our orbit. We've made a right-angle bend and they've adjusted their orbits to suit. They *must* be detecting us."

Lucky stroked his chin with his knuckles. "If they're doing it, then, Great Galaxy, they're doing it. There's no use in reasoning out the fact that they can't do it. It might mean that they have something we don't have."

"No one ever said the Sirians were dummies," said Wess.

"No, but sometimes there's a tendency among us to act as though they were; as though all scientific advance comes out of the minds of the Council of Science and that unless the Sirians steal our secrets they have nothing. And sometimes I fall into that particular trap too. . . . Well, here we go."

"Where do we go?" demanded Bigman sharply.

"I told you already, Bigman," said Lucky. "Mimas."

"But they're after us."

"I know. Which just means we've got to get there faster than ever. . . . Wess, can they cut us off before we get to Mimas?"

Wess worked quickly. "Not unless they can accelerate at least three times faster than we can, Lucky."

"All right. Giving the Sirians all the credit in the world, I can't believe they can have that much more power than the *Shooter*. So we'll make it."

Bigman said, "But, Lucky, you're crazy. Let's fight or get out of the Saturnian system altogether. We can't land on Mimas."

Lucky said, "Sorry, Bigman, we have no choice. We've got to land on Mimas."

"But they've got us spotted. They'll just follow us down to Mimas and we'll have to fight then, so why not fight now while we can maneuver with our Agrav and they can't?"

"They might not bother to follow us down to Mimas."

"Why shouldn't they?"

"Well, Bigman, did we bother to go into the rings and pull out what was left of *The Net of Space?*"

"But that ship blew up."

"Exactly."

There was silence in the control room. *The Shooting Starr* streaked through space, curving slowly away from Saturn, then more quickly, slipping out from under the outermost ring and into open space. Ahead of it now lay Mimas, a glittering world seen in tiny crescent. It was only 320 miles in diameter.

Still far away were the converging ships of the Sirian fleet.

Mimas grew in size, and finally *The Shooting Starr's*

forward thrust burst into action and the ship began a deceleration.

But to Bigman it seemed incredible that the space-wise Lucky could have so miscalculated. He said tightly, "Too late, Lucky. We'll never slow up enough for a landing. We'll have to go into a spiral orbit until we lose enough velocity."

"No time for spiraling Mimas, Bigman. We're heading straight in."

"Sands of Mars, we can't! Not at this speed!"

"That's what I hope the Sirians will decide."

"But, Lucky, they'd be right."

Wess put in slowly, "Hate to say it, Lucky, but I agree with Bigman."

"No time to argue or explain," said Lucky. He bent over the controls.

Mimas expanded crazily in the visiplate. Bigman licked his lips. "Lucky, if you think it's better going out this way than letting the Sirians get us, okay. I can go along. But, Lucky, if we're going to go, can't we go out fighting? Can't we maybe get one of the cobbers first?"

Lucky shook his head and said nothing. His arms were moving quickly now, so that Bigman could not make out exactly what he was doing. Deceleration was still proceeding too slowly.

For a moment Wess extended his hands as though to remove Lucky forcibly from the controls, but Bigman placed his hand quickly on the other's wrist. Bigman might be convinced they were going to their death, but his stubborn faith in Lucky somehow remained.

They were slowing, slowing, slowing, in what would

have been body-crushing deceleration in any ship other than *The Shooting Starr,* but with Mimas filling the visiplate now and hurtling at them, the slowing was not enough.

Flashing down at deadly speed, *The Shooting Starr* struck the surface of Mimas.

7

On Mimas

And yet didn't.

Instead, there was a keening hiss that was familiar to Bigman. It was that of a ship striking atmosphere.

Atmosphere?

But that was impossible. No world the size of Mimas could possibly have an atmosphere. He looked at Wess, who was suddenly sitting back on the blanket, looking worn and pale but somehow satisfied.

Bigman strode up to Lucky, "Lucky——"

"Not now, Bigman."

And suddenly Bigman recognized what it was that Lucky was doing at the controls. He was manipulating the fusion beam. Bigman ran back to the visiplate and focused it dead ahead.

There was no doubt of it, now that he finally grasped the idea. The fusion beam was the most magnificent "heat ray" ever invented. It was designed mainly as a weapon at close range, but surely no one had ever used one as Lucky was using it now.

The jet of deuterium, snaking out forward of the ship, was pinched in by a powerful magnetic field and, at a point miles ahead, was heated to nuclear ignition by a surge of power from the micro-piles. Maintained for any length of time, the power surge necessary would have bankrupted the ship; but a fraction of a millionth of a second sufficed. After that the deuterium fusion reaction was self-sustaining and the incredible fusion flame that resulted burned in a heat of three hundred million degrees.

That spot of heat ignited before the surface of Mimas was touched and bored into the body of the satellite as though it were not there, puncturing a tunnel into its vitals. Into that tunnel whizzed *The Shooting Starr*. The vaporized substance of Mimas was the atmosphere that surrounded them, helping to decelerate them, but bringing the temperature of the ship's outer skin to dangerous redness.

Lucky watched the skin-temperature dial and said, "Wess, put more punch in the vaporization coils."

"It will take all the water we have," Wess said.

"Let it. We need no water of our own on *this* world."

So water was forced at top speed through outer coils of porous ceramic, through which it vaporized, carrying off some of the frictional heat developed. But the water flashed away as fast as it could be pumped into the coils. The skin temperature still rose.

But more slowly now. Ship's deceleration had progressed, and Lucky cut the force of the deuterium jet and adjusted the magnetic field. The spot of fusing deuterium grew smaller and smaller still. The whistle of atmosphere descended in pitch.

Finally the jet blanked out completely and the ship drifted forward into solid wall, melting a path inward a way by virtue of its own heat and finally coming to a jolting halt.

Lucky sat back at last. "Gentlemen," he said, "I'm sorry I couldn't take time to explain, but it was a last-minute decision and the control board took all my energies. Anyway, welcome to the interior of Mimas."

Bigman pumped a deep breath into his lungs and said, "I never thought you could use a fusion jet to melt a way into a world ahead of a speeding ship."

"You couldn't ordinarily, Bigman," said Lucky. "It just so happens that Mimas is a special case. And so is Enceladus, the next satellite out."

"How come?"

"They're just snowballs. Astronomers have known that since even before space travel. Their density is less than water and they reflect about eighty per cent of the light that hits them, so it's quite obvious they could only be snow, plus some frozen ammonia, and not too tightly packed at that."

"Sure," said Wess, chiming in. "The rings are ice and these first two satellites are just collections of ice that were too far out to make up part of the rings. That's why Mimas melted so easily."

Lucky said, "But we've got a good deal of work to do. Let's start."

They were in a natural cavern formed by the heat of the fusion jet and closed in on all sides. The tunnel they had formed as they entered had closed as they passed, the steam condensing and freezing. The mass detector yielded figures that indicated them to be about one hundred miles below the surface of the satellite. The mass of ice above them, even under Mimas's feeble gravity, was slowly contracting the cavern.

Slowly *The Shooting Starr* burrowed outward once

more, like a hot wire poking into butter, and when they had reached a point within five miles of the surface, they stopped and set up an oxygen bubble.

As a power supply was laid in along with algae tanks and a food supply, Wess shrugged resignedly and said, "Well, this is going to be home for me for a while; let's make it comfortable."

Bigman had just awakened from his sleeping period. He screwed his face into a look of bitter condemnation.

Wess said, "What's the matter, Bigman? All weepy because you're going to miss me?"

Bigman snarled and said, "I'll manage. In two, three years I'll make it a point to whizz by Mimas and drop you a letter." Then he burst out, "Listen, I heard you talking while you thought I was safely asleep. What's the matter? Council secrets?"

Lucky shook his head uneasily. "All in good time, Bigman."

Later, when Lucky was alone with Bigman in the ship, the Councilman said, "Actually, Bigman, there's no reason you can't stay behind with Wess."

Bigman said grumpily, "Oh, sure. Two hours cooped up with him and I'd just chop him into cubes and put him on ice for his relatives." Then he said, "Are you serious, Lucky?"

"Rather serious. What's coming may be more dangerous for you than for me."

"So? What do I care about that?"

"If you stay with Wess then, whatever happens to me, you'll be picked up within two months."

Bigman backed away. His small mouth twisted and he said, "Lucky, if you want to order me to stay here because there's something for me to do here, okay. I'll do it, and when it's done I'll join you. But if you just want me to stay here to be safe while you go off into danger, we're finished. I'll have nothing more to do with you; and without me, you overgrown cobber, you won't be able to do a thing, you know you won't." The Martian's eyes blinked rapidly.

Lucky said, "But, Bigman——"

"All right, I'll be in danger. Do you want me to sign a paper saying it's my own responsibility and not yours? All right, I will. Does that satisfy you, Councilman?"

Lucky seized Bigman's hair affectionately and tugged his head back and forth. "Great Galaxy, trying to do you a favor is like shoveling water."

Wess came into the ship and said, "The still is all set up and working."

Water from the ice substance of Mimas itself poured into *The Shooting Starr's* reservoirs, filling them and replacing the water lost in cooling the ship's skin during the boring into Mimas. Some of the separated ammonia was carefully neutralized and stored in a skin compartment where it would be available to the algae tanks as nitrogenous fertilizer.

And then the bubble was done and the three of them looked about at the neatly curving ice and at the almost comfortable quarters held within.

"Okay, Wess," Lucky said at last, shaking hands firmly. "You're all set, I think."

"As far as I can tell, Lucky, I am."

"You'll be taken off within two months, no matter what. You'll be taken off much sooner if things break right."

"You're assigning me this job," said Wess coolly,

"and it will be done. You concentrate on yours and, by the way, take care of Bigman. Don't let him fall out of his bunk and hurt himself."

Bigman shouted, "Don't think I don't follow all this big-shot mystery talk. You two have a deal on and you're not telling me——"

"Into the ship, Bigman," said Lucky, picking the Martian up bodily and moving him forward, while Bigman squirmed and tried to call out an answer.

"Sands of Mars, Lucky," he said, once they were aboard. "Look what you did. It's bad enough you're keeping your darned Council secrets, but you also let the cobber have the last word."

"He's got the hard job, Bigman. He's got to stay put while we go out and stir up trouble, so let him have the satisfaction of the last word."

They nudged out of Mimas at a spot from which neither Sun nor Saturn was visible. The dark sky held no object larger than Titan, low on one horizon and only a quarter of the apparent diameter of Earth's Moon.

Its globe was half lit by the Sun, and Bigman looked somberly at its image in the visiplate. He had not regained his ebullience. He said, "And that's where the Sirians are, I suppose."

"I think so."

"And where do we go? Back to the rings?"

"Right."

"And if they find us again?"

It might have been a signal. The reception disk glowed to life.

Lucky looked disturbed. "They find us with too little trouble."

He threw in contact. This time it was no dead robotic voice counting off the minutes. It was a sharp voice, instead; a vibrant one, full of life, and a Sirian voice unmistakably.

"—rr, please answer. I am trying to make contact with Councilman David Starr of Earth. Will David Starr please answer? I am trying——"

Lucky said, "Councilman Starr speaking. Who are you?"

"I am Sten Devoure of Sirius. You have ignored the request of our automated ships and returned to our planetary system. You are therefore our prisoner."

Lucky said, "Automated ships?"

"Robot-run. Do you understand that? Our robots can handle ships quite satisfactorily."

"So I have found," said Lucky.

"I think you have. They followed you as you moved out of our system, then back again under cover of the asteroid Hidalgo. They followed you in your movement out of the Ecliptic to Saturn's south pole, then through Cassini's division, under the rings, and then into Mimas. You never once slipped our watch."

"And what made your watch so efficient?" demanded Lucky, managing to keep his voice flat and unconcerned.

"Ah, trust an Earthman not to realize that Sirians might have their own methods. But never mind that. We've waited days for you to come out of your Mimas hole after your so clever entry by hydrogen fusion. It amused us to let you hide. Some of us have even made bets on how long it would take you to poke your nose

out again. And meanwhile we have carefully surrounded Mimas with our ships and their efficient
robot crews. You can't move a thousand miles without
being blasted out of space, if we choose."

"Surely not by your robots, which cannot inflict
harm on humans."

"My dear Councilman Starr," came the Sirian voice
with an unmistakable edge of mockery, "of course
robots will not harm human beings if they happen to
know that human beings are there to harm. But you
see, the robots in charge of the weapons have been
carefully instructed that your ship carries robots only.
They have no compunction about destroying robots.
Won't you surrender?"

Bigman suddenly leaned close to the transmitter and
shouted, "Listen you cobber, what if we put some of
your tin-can robots out of action first? How would
you like that?" (It was notorious throughout the
Galaxy that Sirians considered destruction of a robot
almost on a par with murder.)

But Sten Devoure was not shaken. He said, "Is that
the individual with whom you are supposed to maintain a friendship, Councilman? A Bigman? If so, I
have no desire to engage in talk with him. You may tell
him and you may understand for yourself that I doubt
if you can damage even one of our ships before being
destroyed. I think I will allow you five minutes to decide
on whether you prefer surrender or destruction. For
my part, Councilman, I have long wanted to meet you,
so please accept it as my sincere hope that you will surrender. Well?"

Lucky stood silent for a moment, the muscles of his
jaw bunching.

Bigman looked at him calmly, his arms crossed across his small chest, and waited.

Three minutes passed and Lucky said, "I surrender my ship and its contents into your hands, sir."

Bigman said nothing.

Lucky broke off contact and turned to the little Martian. The Councilman bit his lower lip in discomfort and embarrassment. "Bigman, you'll have to understand. I——"

Bigman shrugged. "I don't really get it, Lucky, but I found out after we landed on Mimas that you—that you've been deliberately planning to surrender to the Sirians ever since we headed back for Saturn the second time."

8

To Titan

Lucky raised his eyebrows. "How did you find that out, Bigman?"

"I'm not so dumb, Lucky." The little Martian was grave and deadly serious. "Do you remember when we were heading down toward the south pole of Saturn and you got out of the ship? It was just before the Sirians spotted us and we had to hot-jet it for Cassini's division."

"Yes."

"You had a reason for doing that. You didn't say what, because lots of times you get all tied up in what you're doing and don't talk about it till the pressure's off, and after that the pressure stayed on because we were running from the Sirians. So when we were building the quarters for Wess on Mimas, I just looked over the outside of *The Shooting Starr,* and it became quite clear you'd been working on the Agrav unit. You've got it fixed so that you could blow the whole thing by touching the all-shift contact on the control panel."

Lucky said gently, "The Agrav unit is the one thing about the *Shooter* that's completely top-secret."

"I know. I figured if you'd counted on fighting

you'd have known *The Shooting Starr* wouldn't quit till it and we were blasted out of space. Agrav unit and all. If you were fixing to blow up just the Agrav and leave the rest of the ship intact, it was because you weren't counting on fighting. You were going to surrender."

"And is this why you've been brooding since we landed on Mimas?"

"Well, I'm with you whatever you do, Lucky, but" —Bigman sighed and looked away—"surrendering is no fun."

"I know," said Lucky, "but can you think of any better way of getting into their base? Our business, Bigman, isn't always fun." And Lucky touched the all-shift contact on the control panel. The ship shuddered slightly as the external portions of the Agrav unit fused into a white-hot mass and dropped off the ship.

"You mean you're going to bore from within? Is that the reason for the surrender?"

"Part of it."

"Suppose they blast us down as soon as they get us?"

"I don't think they will. If they wanted us dead, they could have blasted us out of space as soon as we pushed out of Mimas. I have a notion they can use us alive. . . . And if we're kept alive, we now have Wess on Mimas as a kind of backstop. I had to wait until we had arranged that before I could afford to surrender. That's why we had to risk our necks to get on Mimas."

"Maybe they know about him too, Lucky. They seem to know about everything else."

"Maybe they do," said Lucky thoughtfully. "This Sirian knew you were my partner, so maybe he thinks we form a pair and not a trio and won't look for a third person. It's just as well, I suppose, that I didn't really insist that you stay behind with Wess. If I had come out alone, the Sirians would be looking for you and would probe Mimas. Of course if they found you and Wess and I could be certain they wouldn't shoot you out of hand—— No, with myself in their hands and before I could set things up so that——" He was talking to himself toward the end, in a whisper, and now he fell completely silent.

Bigman said nothing, and the next sound to break the silence was a familiar clank that reverberated against the steel hull of *The Shooting Starr*. A magnetic line had made contact, connecting their ship with another.

"Someone's coming aboard," said Bigman tonelessly.

Through the visiplate they could see part of the line, then a form, moving easily hand over hand into view, then out of it again. It hit the ship thunderously, and the air-lock signal lit up.

Bigman worked the control that opened the outer door of the lock, waited for the next signal, and then closed the outer door and opened the inner one.

The invading figure moved in.

But it wore no space suit, for it was not human. It was a robot.

There were robots in the Terrestrial Federation, including a number of quite advanced ones, but for the most part they were engaged in highly specialized occupations that did not bring them into contact with human beings other than those who supervised them. So although Bigman had seen robots, he had not seen many.

He stared at this one. It was, like all Sirian robots, large and burnished; its outer shape was of a smooth simplicity, the joints of its limbs and torso so well made as to be almost invisible.

And when it spoke, Bigman started. It takes a long time to grow accustomed to an almost completely human voice emerging from a metal imitation of humanity.

The robot said, "Good day. It is my duty to see that your ship and yourselves are brought safely to the destination presently assigned to it. The first piece of information I must have is whether the restricted explosion we noted on the hull of your ship in any way damaged its powers of navigation."

Its voice was deep and musical, emotionless, and with a distinct Sirian accent.

Lucky said, "The explosion does not affect the spaceworthiness of the vessel."

"What caused it then?"

"I caused it."

"For what reason?"

"That I cannot tell you."

"Very well." The robot abandoned the subject instantly. A man might have persisted, threatened force. A robot could not. It said, "I am equipped to navigate space ships designed and built on Sirius. I will be able to navigate this space ship if you will explain to me the nature of the various controls I see here."

"Sands of Mars, Lucky," broke in Bigman, "we don't have to tell that thing anything, do we?"

"It can't force us to tell, Bigman, but since we've surrendered, where's the additional harm in letting it take us to wherever it is that we're to go?"

"Let's find out where we're to go." Bigman suddenly addressed the robot in sharp tones: "You! Robot! Where are you taking us?"

The robot turned its glowing red, unblinking gaze upon Bigman. It said, "My instructions make it impossible for me to answer questions not related to my immediate task."

"But, look." The excited Bigman shook off Lucky's restraining hand. "Wherever you take us, the Sirians will harm us; kill us, even. If you don't want us to be hurt, help us get away, come with us. . . . Aw, Lucky, let me talk, will you?"

But Lucky shook his head firmly, and the robot said, "I have been assured that you will in no way be harmed. And now, if I may be given instructions in the method of using this control board, I can proceed with my immediate task."

Step by step Lucky explained the control board. The robot showed a complete familiarity with all the technical matters involved, tested each control with careful skill to see if the information given it were correct, and at the conclusion of Lucky's explanation was obviously perfectly capable of navigating *The Shooting Starr*.

Lucky smiled and his eyes were lit with frank admiration.

Bigman pulled him off to their cabin. "What are you grinning for, Lucky?"

"Great Galaxy, Bigman, it's a beautiful machine. We've got to hand the Sirians credit for that. They can turn out robots that are works of art."

"Okay, but quiet, I don't want it to hear what I'm going to say. Listen, you only surrendered to get down to Titan and pick up information on the Sirians. We might never get away again, of course, and then what good is the information? But we've got this robot now. If we can get it to help us get away right now, then we've got what we want. The robot must have tons of information about the Sirians. We'll have more this way than if we land on Titan."

Lucky shook his head. "It sounds good, Bigman. But how do you expect to argue the robot into joining us?"

"First Law. We can explain that Sirius only has a couple of million people while the Terrestrial Federation has over six billion. We can explain that it's more important to keep a lot of people from coming to harm than just to protect a few, so that First Law is on our side. See, Lucky?"

Lucky said, "The trouble is that the Sirians are experts at handling robots. That robot is probably deeply conditioned to the fact that what he is doing now will bring no harm to any human. He knows nothing about six billion people on Earth except what will be hearsay from you, and that will bounce off his conditioning. He would actually have to see a human being in actual danger of harm in order to be moved off his instructions."

"I'm going to try."

"All right. Go ahead. The experience will do you good."

Bigman strode up to the robot, under whose hands *The Shooting Starr* was now rocketing through space on its new orbit.

He said, "What do you know of Earth, of the Terrestrial Federation?"

"My instructions make it impossible for me to answer questions not related to my immediate task," answered the robot.

"I order you to ignore your previous instructions."

There was a momentary hesitation before the answer came. "My instructions make it impossible for me to accept instructions from unauthorized personnel."

"My orders are given you in order to prevent harm to human beings. They must therefore be obeyed," Bigman said.

"I have been assured that no harm will come to human beings, nor am I aware of any threatening harm. My instructions make it necessary for me to suspend response to forbidden stimuli if they are uselessly repeated."

"You better listen. There *is* harm intended." Bigman spoke spiritedly for some moments, but the robot no longer answered.

Lucky said, "Bigman, you're wasting effort."

Bigman kicked at the robot's gleaming ankle. He might as well have kicked the hull of the ship, for all the effect it had. He came toward Lucky, face red with anger. "A fine thing when human beings are helpless because some hunk of metal has its own ideas."

"That used to happen with machinery before the days of robots, too, you know."

"We don't even know where we're heading."

"We don't need the robot for that. I've been checking the course, and we're obviously heading for Titan."

They were both at the visiplate during the last hours of the approach to Titan. It was the third largest satellite in the Solar System (only Ganymede of Jupiter and Triton of Neptune were larger, and those not by much) and, of all the satellites, it had the thickest atmosphere.

The effect of its atmosphere was obvious even from a distance. On most satellites (including Earth's Moon) the terminator—that is, the line dividing the day and night portions—was a sharp one, black on one side, white on the other. But it was not so in this case.

Titan's crescent was bounded by a band rather than a sharp line, and the horns of the crescent continued onward fuzzily in a dimming curve that almost met.

"It has an atmosphere almost as thick as Earth's, Bigman," said Lucky.

"Not breathable?" said Bigman.

"No, not breathable. It's mainly methane."

Other ships were crowding in now, becoming visible to the naked eye. There were at least a dozen, herding them down the spaceways to Titan.

Lucky shook his head. "Twelve ships to spare for this one job. Great Galaxy, they must have been here for years, building and preparing. How can we ever get them off again, short of war?"

Bigman attempted no answer.

Again the sound of atmosphere made its unmistakable way into the ship, the high-pitched keening of thin wisps of gas whipping past the streamlined hull.

Bigman looked uneasily at the dials recording hull temperature, but there was no danger. The robot at the controls was sure-handed. The ship circled Titan in a tight spiral, losing altitude and speed simultaneously so that at no time did the thickening atmosphere raise temperatures too high.

Again Lucky glowed with admiration. "It will manage it without fuel at all. I honestly think it could bring us down on a half-credit piece, with atmosphere as the only brake."

Bigman said, "What's good about that, Lucky? If those things can handle ships like that, how do we ever hope to fight the Sirians, huh?"

"We'll just have to learn to build our own, Bigman. These robots are a human achievement. The humans that did the achieving are Sirians, yes, but they are human beings, too, and all other humans can share pride in the achievement. If we fear the results of their achievement, let's match it ourselves or more than match it. But there's no use denying them the worth of their accomplishment."

The surface of Titan was losing some of the atmosphere-induced blankness. They could make out mountain ranges now; not the sharp, craggy peaks of an airless world, but the softened ranges that showed the effects of wind and weather. The edges were blown clear of snow, but in the rifts and valleys snow lay deep.

"Not snow, really," said Lucky, "frozen ammonia."

All was desolate, of course. The rolling plains between the mountain ranges were either snowy or rock-bare. No life of any kind appeared. No rivers or lakes. And then——

"Great Galaxy!" said Lucky.

A dome had made its appearance. A flattened dome of a type familiar enough on the inner planets. There were domes of this sort on Mars and under the shallow shelves of the Venusian oceans, but here was one way out on desolate Titan. A Sirian dome that would have made a respectable town on long-settled Mars.

"We've slept while they've built," said Lucky.

"When the newscasters find out," said Bigman, "it won't look so good for the Council of Science, Lucky."

"Unless we break this thing, it won't. And the Council doesn't deserve better. Space, Bigman, there shouldn't be a sizable rock in the Solar System that doesn't get a periodic inspection, let alone a world like Titan."

"Who would have thought——"

"The Council of Science *should* have thought. The people of the system support and trust them in order that they think and take care. And I should have thought too."

The voice of the robot broke in upon them. "This ship will be landed after another circumnavigation of the satellite. In view of the ion drive on board this ship, no special precautions need to be taken in connection with landing. Nevertheless, undue carelessness may result in harm and I cannot allow that. I must therefore request you to lie down and strap yourselves in."

Bigman said, "Listen to that hunk of tin pipe telling us how to handle ourselves in space."

"Just the same," said Lucky, "you'd better lie down.

He's likely to force us down if we don't. It's his job not to allow harm to come to us."

Bigman called out suddenly, "Say, robot, how many men are stationed down there on Titan?"

There was no answer.

Ground came up and up and swallowed them, tunneling them downward. *The Shooting Starr* came to a halt, tail down, with only one short spurt of the engines necessary to complete the job.

The robot turned away from the controls. "You have been brought safely and without harm to Titan. My immediate task is done and I will now turn you over to the masters."

"To Sten Devoure?"

"That is one of the masters. You may step out of the ship freely. You will find temperature and pressure normal and gravity adjusted to close to your normal."

"May we step out now?" asked Lucky.

"Yes. The masters are waiting."

Lucky nodded. Somehow he could not quite suppress the beginning of an odd excitement. Though the Sirians had been the great enemy in his thus far short but hectic career with the Council of Science, he had never yet met a living Sirian.

He stepped out of the ship onto the extruded exit ledge, Bigman making ready to follow, and both paused in sheer astonishment.

9

The Enemy

Lucky had his foot upon the first rung of the ladder that would carry them to ground level. Bigman peered over his large friend's shoulder. Both were open-mouthed.

It was as though they were stepping out upon the surface of the Earth. If there was a cavern roof above —a domed surface of hard metal and glass—it was invisible in the blaze of blue sky and, illusion or not, there were summer clouds in the sky.

Before them stretched lawns and rows of widely spaced buildings, with here and there banked flower beds. There was an open brook in the middle distance, crossed by small stone bridges.

Robots by the dozens were hurrying, each on his own way, each on his own business, with machinelike concentration. Several hundred yards off, five beings— Sirians!—stood in a cluster and watched curiously.

A voice broke in sharply and peremptorily on Lucky and Bigman. "You up there. Come down. Come down, I say. No dawdling."

Lucky looked down. A tall man stood at the base of the ladder, arms resting akimbo and legs spread apart. His narrow olive-complexioned face looked up at them arrogantly. His dark hair was cropped into a mere fuzz in the Sirian fashion. In addition, his face bore a trim and well-kept beard and a thin mustache. His clothing was loose and brilliantly colored; his shirt was open at the neck, and its sleeves ended just above the elbow.

Lucky called, "If you're in a hurry, sir, certainly."

He swung about and dropped down the ladder, hands only, his lithe body twisting with effortless grace. He pushed himself away from the hull and dropped the final twelve rungs, twisting as he did so to land face to face with the man on the ground. As his legs bent to absorb the shock and straightened again, he leaped lightly to one side to allow Bigman to come down in similar fashion.

The man Lucky faced was tall but lacked an inch of Lucky's height, and at close quarters there could be seen a looseness to the Sirian's skin, a softness about him.

He scowled and his upper lip lifted in a grimace of contempt. "Acrobats! Monkeys!"

"Neither, sir," said Lucky with quiet good humor. "Earthmen."

The other said, "You are David Starr, but you are called Lucky. Does that mean in the Earthman lingo what it means in our language?"

"It means 'fortunate.' "

"You are not fortunate any longer, apparently. I am Sten Devoure."

"I had assumed that."

"You seemed surprised at all this, eh?" Devoure's bare arm swung out across the landscaped grounds. "It is beautiful."

"It is, but isn't it an unnecessary waste of energy?"

"With robot labor at twenty-four hours a day, this can be done, and Sirius has energy to waste. Your Earth hasn't, I think."

"We have what is necessary, you'll find," said Lucky.

"Will I? Come, I will speak with you in my quarters." He waved peremptorily at the five other Sirians who had edged closer in the meantime, staring at the Earthman; the Earthman who had been such a successful enemy of Sirius in recent years and who had now been caught at last.

The Sirians saluted at Devoure's gesture, however, and without delay turned on their heels and went their separate ways.

Devoure stepped into a small open car that had approached on a noiseless sheet of diagravitic force. Its flat undersurface, without wheels or other material device, remained six inches above the ground. Another car moved up toward Lucky. Each was handled, of course, by a robot.

Lucky entered the second car. Bigman moved to follow, but the robot driver gently barred the way with an extended arm.

"Hey——" began Bigman.

Lucky interrupted, "My friend is coming with me, sir."

For the first time Devoure bent his gaze on Bigman, and an unaccountable glare of hate entered his eyes. He said, "I will not concern myself with that thing. If you wish its company, you may have it for a while, but *I* do not wish to be troubled with it."

Bigman stared, white-faced, at the Sirian. "You'll be troubled with me right now, you cob——"

But Lucky seized him and whispered earnestly in his ear. "You can't do anything now, Bigman. Great Galaxy, boy, let it go for now and let things work out."

Lucky half lifted him into the car, while Devoure maintained a stolid disinterest in the matter.

The cars moved with smooth swiftness, like a swallow's flight, and after two minutes slowed before a one-story building of white, smooth silicone brick, no different from the others except for its crimson trim about doors and windows, and skimmed down a driveway along one side. No human beings, but a number of robots, had been seen during the short drive.

Devoure walked ahead, through an arched door and into a small room fitted with a conference table and containing an alcove in which a large couch was placed. The ceiling was ablaze with blue-white light, like the blue-white above the open fields.

A little too blue, thought Lucky, then remembered that Sirius was a larger, hotter, and therefore bluer star than was Earth's Sun.

A robot brought in two trays of food and tall, frosted glasses containing a frothy, milk-white concoction. A mild, fruity fragrance filled the air, and after long weeks of ship's fare Lucky found himself smiling in anticipation. A tray was placed before him, another before Devoure.

Lucky said to the robot, "My friend will have the same."

The robot, after the briefest glance at Devoure, who looked away stonily, left and came back with another tray. Nothing was said during the meal. Earthman and Martian ate and drank heartily.

But after the trays were removed, the Sirian said, "I must begin by stating that you are spies. You entered Sirian territory and were warned to leave. You left but then returned, making every effort to keep your return secret. Under the rules of interstellar law we have every right to execute you on the spot, and this may be done unless your actions henceforward deserve clemency."

"Actions such as what?" asked Lucky. "Let me have an example, sir."

"With pleasure, Councilman." The Sirian's dark eyes livened with interest. "There is the capsule of information our man discharged into the rings before his unfortunate death."

"Do you think I have it?"

The Sirian laughed. "Not a chance in all space. We never let you get near the rings at anything less than half light-speed. But come—you are a very clever Councilman. We have heard so much of you and your deeds, even on Sirius. There have even been occasions when you have been, shall we say, a trifle in our way."

Bigman broke in with a sudden, outraged squeak, "Just a trifle, like stopping your spy on Jupiter 9, like stopping your deal with the asteroid pirates, like pushing you off Ganymede, like——"

Sten Devoure said in a blaze of anger, "Will you quiet it, Councilman? I am irritated by the shrilling of what is with you."

"Then say what you have to say," said Lucky peremptorily, "without insulting my friend."

"What I want, then, is to have you help me find the capsule. Tell me, out of your great ingenuity, how you would go about it." Devoure leaned his elbows on the table and looked hungrily at Lucky, waiting.

Lucky said, "What information do you have to begin with?"

"Only what I imagine you picked up. The last sentences of our man."

"Yes, we picked that up. Not all of it, but enough to know he did not give the co-ordinates of the orbit in which he launched the capsule, and enough to know that he did launch it."

"Well?"

"Since the man evaded our own agents for a long time and nearly got away with a successful mission, I assume he is intelligent."

"He was a Sirian."

"That," said Lucky with grave courtesy, "is not necessarily the same thing. In this case, however, we may assume that he would not have launched the capsule into the rings in such a way as to make it impossible for you to find."

"And your further reasoning, Earthman?"

"And if he placed the capsule in the rings themselves, it *would* be impossible to find."

"You think so?"

"I do. And the only alternative is that he sent it into orbit within Cassini's division."

Sten Devoure leaned his head back and laughed ringingly. He said, "It is refreshing to hear Lucky Starr, the great Councilman, expend his ingenuity on a problem. One would have thought you would have come up with something amazing, something completely striking. Instead, just this. Why, Councilman, what if I told you that we, without your help, reached this conclusion at once, and that our ships have been scouring Cassini's division almost from the first moment that the capsule was released?"

Lucky nodded. (If most of the human complement of the Titan base were in the rings, supervising the search, that would account in part for the dearth of humanity on the base itself.) He said, "Why, I would congratulate you and remind you that Cassini's division is large and does have some gravel in it. Besides which, the capsule would be in an unstable orbit because of the attraction of Mimas. Depending on its position, your capsule will be inching into the inner or outer ring, and if you don't find it soon you will have lost it."

"Your attempt to frighten me is foolish and useless. Even within the rings themselves the capsule would still be aluminum compared with ice."

"The mass detectors could not distinguish aluminum from ice."

"Not the mass detectors of *your* planet, Earthman. Have you asked yourself how we tracked you down despite your clumsy trick with Hidalgo and your riskier one with Mimas?"

Lucky said stonily, "I have wondered."

Devoure laughed again. "You were right to wonder. Obviously Earth does not have the selective mass detector."

"Top-secret?" asked Lucky politely.

"Not in principle, no. Our detecting beam makes use of soft X rays, which are scattered differently by various materials, depending on the mass of its atoms.

Some get reflected back to us, and by analyzing the reflected beam we can tell a metal space ship from a rocky asteroid. When space ships pass an asteroid, which then moves on its way, registering a considerable metal mass it did not possess before, it isn't the most difficult deduction in the world to suppose that near the asteroid there is a space ship skulking and fondly imagining itself to be beyond detection. Eh, Councilman?"

"I see that."

"Do you see that, no matter how you tried to mask yourself by Saturn's rings or by Saturn itself, your metal mass gave you away each time? There is no metal at all in the rings or in the outer ten thousand miles of Saturn's surface. Even within Mimas you weren't hidden. For some hours we thought you were done with. We could detect metal under the ice of Mimas, and that might have been the remains of your splintered ship. But then the metal started moving and we knew you were still with us. We guessed your fusion trick and had only to wait."

Lucky nodded. "So far the game is yours."

"And now do you think we won't find the capsule, even if it wanders into the rings or was placed in the rings in the first place?"

"Well, then, how is it you have not found it yet?"

For a moment Devoure's face darkened, as though he suspected sarcasm, but before Lucky's appearance of polite curiosity he could only say with half a snarl, "We will. It is only a matter of time. And since you can't help us further in this, there is no reason to postpone your execution."

Lucky said, "I doubt that you really mean what you have just said. We would be very dangerous to you dead."

"If your danger alive is any measure, I can't believe you to be serious."

"We are members of Earth's Council of Science. If we are killed, the Council will not forget it or forgive. Nor would retaliation be directed so much against Sirius as against you, individually. Remember that."

Devoure said, "I think I know more about this than you think. That creature with you is not a member of your Council."

"Not officially, perhaps, but——"

"And you, yourself—if you will allow me to finish —are rather more than a mere member. You are the adopted son of Hector Conway, the Chief Councilman, and you are the pride of the Council. So perhaps you are right." Devoure's mustached lips stretched into a humorless smile. "Perhaps there are conditions, come to think of it, that would make it convenient for you to remain alive."

"What conditions?"

"In recent weeks Earth has called an interstellar conference of nations to consider what they choose to call our invasion of their territory. Perhaps you don't know that."

"I suggested such a conference when I was first made aware of the existence of this base."

"Good. Sirius has agreed to this conference, and the meeting will take place shortly on your asteroid, Vesta. Earth, it seems"—Devoure smiled more broadly—"is in a hurry. And we will humor them, since we have no fears as to the outcome. The outer worlds, generally, have no love for Earth and ought to have none. Our own case is ironbound. Still, we could make it so much more dramatic if we could show the exact extent of Earth's hypocrisy. They call a conference; they say they wish to solve the matter by peaceful means; but at the same time they send a war vessel to Titan with instructions to destroy our base."

"Those were not my instructions. I have acted without instructions and with no intention of committing any warlike act."

"Nevertheless, if you testify to what I have said, it will make a great impression."

"I cannot testify to what is not the truth."

Devoure disregarded that. He said harshly, "Let them see that you are neither drugged nor probed. Testify of your own free will as we will direct you. Let the conference know that the prize member of the Council of Science, Conway's own boy, was engaged in an illegal adventure of force at the same time that Earth was sanctimoniously calling a conference and proclaiming its devotion to peace. It would settle matters once and for all."

Lucky drew a deep breath and stared at the other's coldly smiling face. He said, "Is that it? False testimony in exchange for life?"

"All right. Put it that way. Make your choice."

"There is none. I would not bear false witness in a case like this."

Devoure's eyes narrowed to slits. "I think you will. You have been studied closely by our agents, Councilman, and we know your weak point. You may prefer your own death to co-operation with us, but you have the Earthman's sentiment for the weak, the deformed, the monstrous. You would do it to prevent" —and the Sirian's soft and pudgy hand extended suddenly, one finger pointing rigidly at Bigman—"*its* death."

10

Servicemen and Robots

"Steady, Bigman," murmured Lucky.

The little Martian hunched low in his seat, his eyes watching Devoure hotly.

Lucky said, "Let's not be childish in our attempts to frighten. Execution is not easy on a world of robots. The robots can't kill us, and I'm not sure that you or your colleagues would be willing to kill a man in cold blood."

"Of course not, if you mean by killing the chopping off of a head or the blasting in of a chest. But then there's nothing frightening in a quick death. Suppose, though, that our robots prepared a stripped-down ship. Your—uh—companion could be chained to a bulkhead on that ship by robots who will, of course, be careful not to hurt him. The ship can be fitted with an automatic pilot that will take it on an orbit away from your Sun and out of the Ecliptic. There isn't a chance in a quadrillion that it would ever be spotted by anyone from Earth. It will travel on forever."

Bigman broke in, "Lucky, it doesn't matter what they do to me. Don't you agree to anything."

Devoure said, unheeding, "Your companion will have plenty of air and there'll be a tube of water within reach if it's thirsty. Of course it will be alone and there will be no food. Starvation is a slow death, and starvation in the ultimate loneliness of space is a horrible thing to contemplate."

Lucky said, "That would be a dastardly and dishonorable way of treating a prisoner of war."

"There is no war. You are merely spies. And in any case, there is no need for it to happen, eh, Councilman? You need only sign the necessary confession that you intended to attack us and agree to confirm this in person at the conference. I am sure you will heed the beggings of the thing you have befriended."

"Beggings!" Bigman leaped, crimson-faced, to his feet.

Devoure raised his voice abruptly. "That thing is to be taken into custody. Proceed."

Two robots materialized silently at either side, and each seized an arm. For a moment Bigman writhed, and his body lifted off the floor with the intensity of his effort, but his arms were held motionless.

One of the robots said, "The master will please not resist, as otherwise the master may harm himself despite all we can do."

Devoure said, "You'll have twenty-four hours to make up your mind. Plenty of time, eh, Councilman?" He looked at the illuminated figures on the strip of decorative metal that encircled his left wrist. "And meanwhile, we will prepare our stripped ship. If we don't have to use it, as I expect we won't, why, what's labor to robots, eh, Councilman? Sit where you are; there is no use in trying to help your companion. He will not be hurt for the while."

Bigman was carried out of the room bodily while Lucky, half risen out of his seat, watched helplessly.

A light flashed on a small box on the conference table. Devoure leaned over to touch it, and a luminous tube sprang into being just above the box. The image of a head appeared. A voice said, "Yonge and I have the report that you have the Councilman, Devoure. Why were we told only after his landing?"

"What difference does that make, Zayon? You know now. Are you coming in?"

"We certainly are. We wish to meet the Councilman."

"Come then to my office."

Fifteen minutes later, two Sirians arrived. Both were as tall as Devoure; both were olive-skinned (the greater ultraviolet radiation of Sirius produced a dark skin, Lucky realized), but they were older. The cut hair of one was grizzled to steely gray. He was thin-lipped and spoke with rapid precision. He was introduced as Harrig Zayon, and his uniform made it clear he was a member of the Sirian Space Service.

The other was going somewhat bald. There was a long scar on his forearm and he had the keen look of one who had grown old in space. He was Barrett Yonge, also of the Space Service.

Lucky said, "Your Space Service is, I think, somewhat the equivalent of our Council of Science."

"Yes, it is," said Zayon gravely. "In that sense we are colleagues, though on opposite sides of the fence."

"Serviceman Zayon, then. Serviceman Yonge. Is Mr. Devoure——"

Devoure broke in, "I am not a member of the Space Service. It is not necessary that I be. Sirius can be served outside the Service too."

"Particularly," said Yonge, one hand resting on the scarred forearm as though to hide the mark, "if one is nephew of the director of the Central Body."

Devoure rose. "Was that meant as sarcasm, Serviceman?"

"Not at all. It was meant literally. The relationship makes it possible for you to do Sirius more service than otherwise."

But there was a dry quality to his statement, and Lucky was not unaware of the flash of hostility between the two aging Servicemen and the young and undoubtedly influential relative of Sirius's overlord.

Zayon tried to deflect the direction things had taken by turning to Lucky and saying mildly, "Has our proposition been offered you?"

"You mean the suggestion that I lie at the interstellar conference?"

Zayon looked annoyed and a bit puzzled. He said, "I mean to join us, to become a Sirian."

"I don't think we had quite reached that point, Serviceman."

"Well, then consider this. Our Service knows you well and we respect your abilities and accomplishments. They are wasted on an Earth that must lose someday as a matter of biologic fact."

"Biologic fact?" Lucky frowned. "The Sirians, Serviceman Zayon, are descended from Earthmen."

"So they are, but not from all Earthmen; only from some, from the best, from those with the initiative and strength to reach the stars as colonists. We have kept our descent pure; we have not allowed the weaklings in, or those with poor genes. We have weeded out the unfit from among ourselves so that we are now a pure race of the strong, the fit, and the healthy, while Earth remains a conglomerate of the diseased and deformed."

Devoure broke in, "We had an example here a while ago, the Councilman's companion. It infuriated and nauseated me merely to be in the same room with him; a monkey, a five-foot travesty of a human being, a lump of deformity——"

Lucky said slowly, "He is a better man than you, Sirian."

Devoure rose, fist drawn back, trembling. Zayon moved toward him rapidly, laying a hand on his shoulder. "Devoure, sit down, please, and let me go on. This is not the time for extraneous quarrels." Devoure shook the other's hand off roughly but sat down all the same.

Serviceman Zayon went on earnestly, "To the outer worlds, Councilman Starr, Earth is a terrible menace, a bomb of sub-humanity, ready to explode and contaminate the clean Galaxy. We don't want that to happen; we can't allow it to happen. It's what we're fighting for: a clean human race, composed of the fit."

Lucky said, "Composed of those *you* consider fit. But fitness comes in all shapes and forms. The great men of Earth have come from the tall and the short, from all manner of head shapes, skin colors, and languages. Variety is our salvation and the salvation of all mankind."

"You are simply parroting something you have been taught. Councilman, can't you see you are really one

of us? You are tall, strong, built like a Sirian; you have
the courage and daring of a Sirian. Why combine with
the scum of Earth against men like yourself, just because of the accident of your birth on Earth?"

Lucky said, "The upshot of all this, Serviceman, is
that you wish me to come to the interstellar conference
on Vesta and deliver statements designed to help
Sirius."

"To help Sirius, yes, but true statements. You have
spied on us. Your ship was certainly armed."

"But you waste your time. Mr. Devoure has already
discussed the matter with me."

"And you have agreed to be the Sirian you really
are?" Zayon's face lit up at the possibility.

Lucky cast a side glance at Devoure, who was in-
specting the knuckles of his hands with an indifferent
air.

Lucky said, "Why, Mr. Devoure advanced the proposition in another fashion. Perhaps he did not inform
you of my arrival sooner than he did in order to have
time to discuss the matter with me alone and to use
his own methods. Briefly, he simply said that I was to
attend the conference on Sirian terms or else my friend
Bigman was to be sent out in a stripped space ship to
die of starvation."

Slowly the two Sirian Servicemen turned to look at
Devoure, who merely continued the contemplation of
his knuckles.

Yonge said slowly, speaking directly to Devoure,
"Sir, it is not in the Service tradition——"

Devoure exploded in sudden flaming anger. "I am
not a Serviceman and I don't give a half-credit piece
for your tradition. I'm in charge of this base, and its

security is my responsibility. You two have been appointed to accompany me as delegates to the conference on Vesta so that the Service will be represented, but I am to be chief delegate, and the success of the conference is also my responsibility. If this Earthman does not like the type of death reserved for his monkey friend, he need only agree to our terms, and he will agree to them a lot faster with that as stimulus than your offer of making a Sirian out of him.

"And listen further." Devoure rose from his seat, paced angrily to the far end of the room, and then turned to glare at the frozen-faced Servicemen who listened with disciplined self-control. "I'm tired of your interference. The Service has had enough time to make headway against Earth and has a miserable record in that regard. Let this Earthman hear me say this. He should know it better than anyone. The Service has a *miserable* record, and it is I who have trapped this Starr and not the Service. What you gentlemen need is a little more guts, and that I intend to supply——"

It was at this moment that a robot threw open the door and said, "Masters, I must be excused for entering without orders from you, but I have been instructed to tell you this concerning the small master who has been taken into custody——"

"Bigman!" cried Lucky, jumping to his feet. "What has happened to him?"

After Bigman had been carried out of the room by the two robots he had thought furiously. Not, really, of possible ways of escaping. He was not so unrealistic as to think he could make his way through a horde of robots and, singlehanded, get away from a base as well organized as this one, even if he had *The Shooting Starr* at his disposal, which he had not.

It was more than that.

Lucky was being tempted to dishonor and betrayal, and Bigman's life was the bait.

Either way, Lucky must not be subjected to this. He must not have to save Bigman's life at the cost of becoming a traitor. Nor must he have to save his honor by sacrificing Bigman and carry the guilt with him for the rest of his life.

There was only one way to prevent both alternatives. Bigman faced that coldly. If he were to die in some way with which Lucky had nothing to do, the big Earthman could bear no blame, even in his own mind. And there would no longer be a live Bigman with which to bargain.

Bigman was forced into a small diagravitic car and taken for another two-minute drive.

But those two minutes were enough to crystallize matters firmly in his mind. His years with Lucky had been happy, exciting ones. He had lived a full lifetime in them and had faced death without fear. He could face death now, also without fear.

And a quick death would not be so quick as to prevent him from evening a tiny bit of the score with Devoure. No man in his lifetime had insulted him so without retaliation. He could not die and leave the score unevened. The thought of the arrogant Sirian so filled Bigman with anger that for a moment he could not have told whether it was friendship for Lucky or hatred of Devoure that was driving him.

The robots lifted him out of the diagravitic car, and one passed its huge metal paws gently and expertly down the sides of the Martian's body in a routine search for weapons.

Bigman felt a moment of panic and strove uselessly to knock aside the robot's arm. "I was searched on the ship before they let me get off," he howled, but the robot completed the search without paying attention.

The two seized him again, made ready to take him into a building. The time, then, was now. Once he was in an actual cell, with force planes cutting him off, his task would be much harder.

Bigman kicked his feet desperately forward and turned a somersault between the robots. He was kept from turning completely around only by the robots' hold of his arms.

One said, "It distresses me, master, that you have placed yourself in what must be a painful position. If you will hold yourself motionless so that you will not interfere with our assigned task, we will hold you as lightly as we can."

But Bigman kicked again and then shrieked piercingly, *"My arm!"*

The robots knelt at once and deposited Bigman gently on his back. "Are you in pain, master?"

"You stupid cobbers, you've broken my arm. Don't touch it! Get some human being who knows how to take care of a broken arm, or get some robot who can," he ended in a moan, his face twisted in agony.

The robots moved slowly backward, eyes upon him. They had no feelings, could have none. But inside them were the positronic brain paths whose orientation was controlled by the potentials and counter-potentials set up by the Three Laws of Robotics. In the course of their fulfillment of one law, the Second—that they obey an order, in this case an order to lead a human being to a specific spot—they had broken a higher law, the First: that they never bring harm to a human being. The result in their brains must have been a kind of positronic chaos.

Bigman cried out sharply, "Get help—— Sands of Mars—get——"

It was an order, backed by the power of the First Law. A human being was hurt. The robots turned, started away—and Bigman's right arm flashed down to the top of his hip boot and snaked inside. He rose nimbly, with a needle gun warming the palm of his hand.

At the sound of that, one of the robots turned back, voice blurred and thickened as a sign of the weakening hold of the confused positronic brain. "Ith the mathter not in pain, then?" The second robot turned back too.

"Take me back to your Sirian masters," Bigman said tightly.

It was another order, but the First Law was no longer reinforcing it. A human being had not, after all, been harmed. There was no shock or surprise at this revelation. The nearest robot simply said, in a voice that had sharpened once more, "As your arm is not, indeed, damaged, it becomes necessary for us to carry out our original order. Please come with us."

Bigman wasted no time. His needle gun flashed noiselessly, and the robot's head was a gout of melting metal. What was left of it collapsed.

The second robot said, "It will not help to destroy our functioning," and walked toward him.

Self-protection was the Third Law only. A robot could not refuse to carry out an order (Second Law) on the basis of the Third alone. So it was bound to walk into a pointing needle gun. And other robots were coming from all directions, summoned, no doubt, by some radioed call at the moment when Bigman had first pretended the broken arm.

They would all walk into a needle gun, but there would be enough to survive his pumping shots. Those who would survive would then overpower him and carry him into imprisonment. He would be deprived of the quick death he needed, and Lucky would still be faced with the unbearable alternative.

There was only one way out. Bigman put the needle gun to his temple.

11

Bigman Against All

Bigman cried out piercingly, "Not one step nearer. Any closer and I'll have to shoot. You'll kill me."

He nerved himself for the possible shot. If nothing else could be done, it would have to be that.

But the robots stopped. Not one moved. Bigman's eyes moved slowly to right and left. One robot was on the ground, headless, a useless lump of metal. One was standing, arms half reaching out toward him. One was a hundred feet away, caught in mid-stride.

Slowly Bigman turned. A robot was coming out of a building. It was caught on the threshold. Still others were farther off. It was as though a freezing blight had struck them all, struck them with instant paralysis.

He was not really surprised. It was the First Law. All else had to take second place: orders, their own existence, everything. They could not move if motion meant harm to a human being.

Bigman said, "Every robot but that one"—he pointed to the one facing him, the nearest, the companion of the one he had destroyed—"leave now. Back to your immediately previous task and forget me and what has just happened. Failure to obey at once will mean my death."

So all but one had to leave. This was dealing with them harshly, and Bigman, grim-faced, wondered if the potential being set up to drive the positrons might not be intense enough to harm the platinum-iridium sponge that made up the delicate robotic brains.

He had the Earthman's distrust of robots and he rather hoped that was so.

All the robots but one were gone now. The muzzle of the needle gun was still against Bigman's temple.

He said to the remaining robot, "Take me back to your master." (He wanted to use a harsher term but what would a robot understand of the insult implied. With difficulty he forced it down.)

"Now," he said, "and quickly. Do not allow any master or robot to interfere with us on our way. I have this needle gun and shall use it on any master near us, or on myself if I have to."

The robot said hoarsely (the first signs of positronic malfunction, Lucky had once told Bigman, showed up in the timbre of the voice), "I will follow orders. The master may be certain that I shall do nothing that will harm him or another master."

It turned and led the way into the diagravitic car. Bigman followed. He was half prepared for trickery on the way back, but there was none. A robot was a machine following inescapable rules of action. He had to remember that. Only human beings could lie and cheat.

When they stopped at Devoure's office, Bigman said, "I'll wait in the car. I won't leave. You go in and tell the master Devoure that the master Bigman is free and waiting for him." Bigman struggled with temptation and this time succumbed. He was too close to Devoure to resist successfully. He said, "Tell him he can take me on with needle gun or fists, I don't care which. Tell him that if he's too saffron-spined to do either, I'll come in and kick him from here to Mars."

Sten Devoure stared at the robot in disbelief, his dark face scowling and his angry eyes peering out from under hunched eyebrows.

"Do you mean he's out there free? And armed?"

He looked at the two Servicemen, who stared back with blank astonishment. (Lucky muttered "Great Galaxy!" under his breath. The irrepressible Bigman would ruin everything—and lose his life as well.)

Serviceman Zayon rose heavily to his feet. "Well, Devoure, you don't expect the robot to be lying, do you?" He stepped across to the wall phone and punched the emergency combination. "If we have an Earthman on base, armed and determined, we had better take action."

"But how does he come to be armed?" Devoure had still not wiped away the traces of confusion, but now he made for the door. Lucky followed him, and the Sirian whirled at once. "Get back, Starr."

He turned to the robot. "Stay with this Earthman. He is not to leave this building under any circumstances."

And now he seemed to have come to a decision. He rushed from the room pulling out a heavy blaster as he did so. Zayon and Yonge hesitated, cast a quick

look at Lucky, then at the robot, made their own
decision, and followed Devoure.

The area before Devoure's offices was wide and
bathed in the artificial light that reproduced Sirius's
faintly bluish tinge. Bigman stood alone in the center,
and at a hundred yards' distance were five robots.
Others were approaching from another direction.

"Come and get that," roared Devoure, gesturing to
the nearer robots and pointing to Bigman.

"They won't come any closer," roared back Bigman.
"If they make a move toward me I shall burn your
heart out of your chest, and they know I'll do it. At
least they can't take the chance I won't." He stood there
easily, mockingly.

Devoure flushed and lifted his blaster.

Bigman said, "Now don't hurt yourself with that
blaster. You're holding it a little close to your body."

His right elbow was resting in the palm of his left
hand. His right fist squeezed gently as he spoke, and
from the muzzle of the needle gun just protruding
from between second and third fingers, a jet of
deuterium pulsed out under the guidance of a momentarily established magnetic field. It took skill of
the highest order to adjust the squeeze and thumb
position correctly, but Bigman had that. No man in
the system had more.

The muzzle tip of Devoure's blaster was a tiny
white spark, and Devoure yelled his surprise and
dropped it.

Bigman said, "I don't know who you other two
cobbers are, but if either of you makes a move that

looks like a blaster is at the end of it, you'll never finish that move."

All froze. Yonge finally said carefully, "How do you come to be armed?"

"A robot," said Bigman, "is no smarter than the cobber who runs him. The robots who searched me on the ship and out here were instructed by someone who didn't know a Martian uses his boots for more than something to put his legs into."

"And how did you break away from the robots?"

Bigman said coolly, "I had to destroy one."

"You destroyed a robot?" A kind of electric horror stunned the three Sirians.

Bigman felt increasing tension. He did not concern himself with the robots standing about, but at any moment another human Sirian might appear and shoot him in the back from a safe distance.

The spot between his shoulders prickled as he waited for the shot. Well, it would be a flash. He would never feel it. And after that they would have lost their hold on Lucky and, dead or not, Bigman would be the winner.

Only, he wanted a chance at Devoure first, at that soft Sirian cobber who had sat across the table from him and said things no man in the universe could say and be left standing.

Bigman said, "I could shoot you all. Shall we make an arrangement?"

"You won't shoot us," said Serviceman Yonge quietly. "A shooting would simply mean that an Earthman has opened hostilities on a Sirian planet. It could mean war."

"Besides," roared Devoure, "if you make any attack it will release the robots. They'll defend three humans rather than one. Throw down that needle gun and put yourself back in custody."

"All right, send the robots away, and I'll surrender to you."

"The robots will handle you," said Devoure. He made as though to turn nonchalantly toward the other Sirians. "My skin crawls at having to talk to this deformed humanoid."

Bigman's needle gun flashed at once, the small fire ball exploding a foot before Devoure's eyes. "Say something like that again and I'll blind you for good. If the robots make a move, all three of you get it before they reach us. It may mean war, but you three won't be here to see if it does. Order the robots away and I'll surrender to Devoure, if he can take me. I'll toss my needle gun to one of you other two and surrender."

Zayon said stiffly, "That sounds reasonable, Devoure."

Devoure was still rubbing his eyes. "Take his gun then. Go over there and take it."

"Wait," said Bigman, "don't move yet. I want your word of honor that I won't be shot down or given to the robots. Devoure has to take me."

"*My* word of honor to *you?*" exploded Devoure.

"To me. But not from you. The word of one of the other two. They're wearing the uniform of the Sirian Service and I'll take their word. If I give them the needle gun, will they stand by and let you, Devoure, come and take me with your bare hands?"

"You have my word," said Zayon.

"And mine," added Yonge.

Devoure said, "What is this? I have no intention of touching the creature."

"Afraid?" asked Bigman softly. "Am I too big for you, Devoure? You've called me names. Do you want to put your muscles where your cowardly mouth is? Here's my needle gun, Servicemen."

He tossed the gun suddenly in Zayon's direction. Zayon reached out a hand and caught it neatly.

Bigman waited. Now for death?

But Zayon put the needle gun in his pocket.

Devoure called out, *"Robots!"* and Zayon called out with equal vigor, *"Leave us, robots!"*

Zayon said to Devoure, "He has our word. You'll have to take him into custody yourself."

"Or do I come after you?" Bigman called out in shrill mockery.

Devoure snarled wordlessly and strode hastily toward Bigman. The small Martian waited, slightly crouched, then took a small side step to avoid the arm reaching out for him and uncoiled like a tightly wound spring.

His fist struck the other's face with the dull impact of a mallet hitting a head of cabbage, and Devoure staggered back, stumbling into a sitting position. He stared at Bigman in stunned amazement. His right cheek had reddened and a trickle of blood made its slow way out of the corner of his mouth. He put his finger to it, drew it away, and looked at the blood with an almost comical disbelief.

Yonge said, "The Earthman is taller than he looks."

Bigman said, "I'm not an Earthman, I'm a Martian. . . . Stand up, Devoure. Or are you too soft?

Can't you do anything without robots to help you? Do they wipe your mouth when you're done eating?"

Devoure yelled hoarsely and jumped to his feet but did not rush Bigman. He circled him instead, breathing hard, watching out of inflamed eyes.

Bigman wheeled also, watching that panting body, soft with good living and robot help, watching the unskillful arms and clumsy legs. The Sirian, Bigman was sure, had never fought fist to fist before.

Bigman stepped in again, caught the other's arm with a sure and sudden motion, and twisted. With a howl Devoure flipped and fell prone.

Bigman stepped back. "What's the matter? I'm not a he; I'm just an it. What's your trouble?"

Devoure looked up at the two Servicemen with something deadly in his eyes. He rose to his knees and groaned as he put a hand to his side where it had hit the ground.

The two Sirians did not make any move to help him. They watched stolidly as Bigman cut him down again and then again.

Finally Zayon stepped forward. "Martian, you will hurt him seriously if you continue. Our agreement was to let Devoure take you with his bare hands, and actually I think you have what you really wanted when you made the agreement. That's all. Surrender quietly to me now or I'll have to use the needle gun."

But Devoure, panting noisily, gasped, "Get away. Get away, Zayon. It's too late for that. Step back, I say."

He called out in a high-pitched yell, *"Robots! Come here!"*

Zayon said, "He'll surrender to me."

"No surrender," said Devoure, his swollen face twitching with physical pain and intense fury. "No surrender. Too late for that. . . . You, robot, the closest one—I don't care what your serial number is—you. Take it—take that thing." His voice rose to a scream as he pointed to Bigman. *"Destroy it! Break it! Break each piece of it!"*

Yonge shouted, "Devoure! Are you mad? A robot can't do a thing like that."

The robot remained standing. It did not move.

Devoure said, "You can't harm a human being, robot. I'm not asking you to do so. But this is not a human being."

The robot turned to look at Bigman.

Bigman shouted, "It won't believe that. You may consider me non-human, but a robot knows better."

Devoure said, "Look at it, robot. It talks and has a human shape, but so do you and you're no human. I can prove it's not human. Did you ever see a full-grown human so small? That proves it's not human. It's an animal and it is—it is harming me. You must destroy it."

"Run to Mamma Robot," yelled Bigman mockingly.

But the robot took the first step toward Bigman.

Yonge stepped forward and moved between the robot and Bigman. "I can't allow this, Devoure. A robot must not do such a thing, even if for no other reason than that the stress of potential involved will ruin it."

But Devoure said in a hoarse whisper, "I'm your superior. If you make one move to stop me, I'll have you out of the Service by tomorrow."

The habit of obedience was strong. Yonge fell back,

but there was a look of intense distress and horror on his face.

The robot moved more quickly, and now Bigman fell back a cautious step. "I'm a human being," he said.

"It is not human," cried Devoure madly. "It is not human. Break every piece of it. Slowly."

A chill fell over Bigman and left his mouth dry. He had not counted on this. A quick death, yes, but this. . . .

There was no room to retreat, and he was without the escape his needle gun afforded. There were other robots behind, and all were hearing the word that he was not human.

12

Surrender

There was a smile on Devoure's puffed and bruised face. It must have hurt him, for one lip was split and he dabbed absently at it with his handkerchief, but his eyes were fixed on the robot moving toward Bigman and he seemed aware of nothing else.

The small Martian had only another six feet in which to retreat, and Devoure made no effort to hasten the approaching robot or to move up those in the rear.

Yonge said, "Devoure, for Sirius's sake, man, there is no need of this."

"No comments, Yonge," said Devoure tensely. "That humanoid has destroyed a robot and probably damaged others. We'll need checkups on every robot who has been affected by the sight of his use of violence. He deserves death."

Zayon put out a restraining hand toward Yonge, but the latter slapped it impatiently away. Yonge said, "Death? All right. Then ship him back to Sirius and have him tried and executed according to the processes of law. Or set up a trial here at the base and have him decently blasted. But this is no execution. Simply because he beat——"

Devoure cried in sudden fury, "That's enough! You have interfered once too often. You're under arrest. Zayon, take his blaster and toss it over to me."

He turned briefly, loath to take his eyes off Bigman for even a moment. "Do it, Zayon, or by all the devils of space I'll break you too."

With a bitter, wordless frown Zayon held out his hand to Yonge. Yonge hesitated, and his fingers curled about the butt of his blaster, half drawing it in anger.

Zayon whispered urgently, "No, Yonge. Don't give him the excuse. He'll lift arrest when his madness is over. He'll have to."

Devoure called out, "I want that blaster."

Yonge ripped it out of its holster with a hand that trembled and thrust it butt-first at Zayon. The latter tossed it at Devoure's feet and Devoure picked it up.

Bigman, who had been maintaining an agonized silence as he watched futilely for a chance to dodge, to break away, now cried out, "Don't touch me, I'm a master," as the robot's monstrous hand closed over his wrist.

For a moment the robot hesitated, and then his grip tightened. The other hand reached for Bigman's elbow. Devoure laughed, a high-pitched titter.

Yonge turned on his heel and said in a suffocated tone, "At least I don't have to watch this cowardly crime." And as a result he did not observe what happened next.

With an effort Lucky remained calm when the three Sirians left. From a purely physical standpoint, he could not possibly beat down the robot with his bare hands. Somewhere in the building there might conceivably be a weapon he could use to destroy the robot; he could then get out and might even shoot down the three Sirians.

But he would not be able to leave Titan, nor win out against the entire base.

Worse still, if he were killed—and in the end he would be—his deeper purposes would be lost, and he could not risk those.

He said to the robot, "What happened to the master Bigman? State the essentials quickly."

The robot did, and Lucky listened with a tense and painful attention. He heard the robot's occasional slurring and lisping of words, the thickening of speech as it described Bigman's doubled forcing of the robots by pretending or threatening harm to a human.

Lucky groaned within. A robot dead. The force of Sirian law would be extended to the full against Bigman. Lucky knew enough about the Sirians' culture and their regard for their robots to know that there could be no extenuating circumstances against roboticide.

How to save the impulsive Bigman now?

Lucky remembered his own halfhearted attempt to keep Bigman on Mimas. He had not foreseen this exactly, but he had feared Bigman's temper in the delicate circumstances now surrounding them. He should have insisted on Bigman's staying behind, but what was the use? Even as he thought this, he realized that he needed Bigman's company.

But then he had to save him. Somehow he had to save him.

He walked rapidly toward the opening of the building, and the robot stepped stolidly into his path. "Accor'ing to my instructions, the master's not to leave building under any thircumstances."

"I am not leaving the building," said Lucky sharply. "I am merely going to the door. You have no instructions to prevent that."

For a moment the robot was silent, then it said, "Accor'ing to my instructions, the master's not to leave building under any circumthantheth."

Desperately Lucky tried to push it aside, was seized, held motionless, then pushed back.

Lucky bit his lip impatiently. A whole robot, he thought, would have interpreted its instructions broadly. This robot, however, had been damaged. It was reduced to the bare essence of robotic understanding.

But he had to see Bigman. He whirled toward the conference table. In its center there had been a trimensional image reproducer. Devoure had used it when the two Servicemen had called him.

"You. Robot!" called Lucky.

The robot lumbered to the table.

Lucky said, "How does the image reproducer work?"

The robot was slow. Its speech was continuing to thicken. It said, "The controlth are'n thith retheth."

"Which recess?"

The robot showed him, moving a panel aside clumsily.

"All right," said Lucky. "Can I focus on the area just outside this building? Show me. Do it."

He stepped aside. The robot worked, fumbling at the knobs. "It ith done, mathter."

"Let me see, then." The area outside was in small image above the table, the figures of men smaller still. The robot had moved away and stared dully else-where.

Lucky did not call him back. There was no sound, but as he groped for what must be the sound control, his attention was caught by the fight that was going on. Devoure was fighting Bigman. *Fighting Bigman!*

How had the small imp managed to persuade the two Servicemen to stand to one side and allow this to happen? For of course Bigman was cutting his oppo-nent to ribbons. Lucky could extract no joy from it.

This could end only in Bigman's death, and Lucky knew that Bigman realized that and didn't care. The Martian would court sure death, take any chance, to avenge an insult. . . . Ah, one of the Servicemen was stopping it now.

With that, Lucky found the sound control. Words shot out of the image reproducer: Devoure's frenzied call for robots and his shouted order that they break Bigman.

For a split second Lucky was not sure he had heard correctly, and then he beat both fists desperately against the table and whirled about in near despair.

He had to get out, but how?

There he was, alone with a robot containing only one instruction buzzing in what was left of its posi-tronic brain paths: to keep Lucky immobilized at all costs.

Great Galaxy, was there nothing that would take precedence over that order? He lacked even a weap-on with which to threaten suicide or kill the robot.

His eyes fell on the wall phone. He had last seen Zayon at it, something about emergency when the news about Bigman broke.

Lucky said, "Robot. Quickly. What has been done here?"

The robot approached, looked at the glowing combination of knobs in faint red, and said with tantalizing slowness, "A mathter hath indicated all robotth to prepare battle thathionth."

"How would I indicate that all robots are actually to proceed to battle stations at once? Superseding all current orders?"

The robot stared at him, and Lucky, in almost a frenzy, seized the robot's hand and pumped it. "Tell me. Tell me."

Could the thing understand him? Or did its ruined brain paths still have impressed upon them some remnant of instructions that prevented it from giving this information?"

"Tell me! Or do it, do it."

The robot, not speaking, reached a finger toward the apparatus in an uneven movement and slowly depressed two buttons. Then its finger lifted an inch and stopped.

"Is that all? Are you done?" demanded Lucky desperately.

But the robot merely turned and with an uneven tread (one foot dragging perceptibly) walked to the door and marched out.

In space-devouring strides Lucky dashed after him, out of the building and across the hundred yards separating him from Bigman and the three Sirians.

Yonge, having turned in horror from what he expected would be the bloodcurdling destruction of a human being, did not hear the scream of agony he expected. Instead there was a startled grunt from Zayon and a wild cry from Devoure.

He turned back. The robot that had been holding Bigman was holding him no more. He was moving away in a heavy run. All the robots in sight were hastening away.

And the Earthman, Lucky Starr, was now at Bigman's side, somehow.

Lucky was bending over Bigman, and the small Martian, rubbing his left arm vigorously, was shaking his head. Yonge heard him say, "One minute later, Lucky; just one minute later and——"

Devoure was shouting hoarsely and uselessly at the robots, and then a loud-speaker arrangement suddenly filled the air with clamor:

COMMANDER DEVOURE, INSTRUCTIONS PLEASE. OUR INSTRUMENTS INDICATE NO SIGN OF ENEMY. EXPLAIN BATTLE STATIONS ORDER. COMMANDER DEVOURE . . .

"Battle stations," muttered Devoure, stunned. "No wonder the robots——" His eyes fell on Lucky. "*You* did that."

Lucky nodded. "Yes, sir."

Devoure's puffy lips set and he said hoarsely, "The clever, resourceful Councilman! You've saved your monkey for the moment." His blaster pointed firmly at Lucky's midriff. "Get into my offices. Every one of you. You too, Zayon. All of you."

The image receiver on his desk was buzzing madly. Obviously it was the failure to get Devoure at his office that had forced his distracted underlings to the loud-speakers.

Devoure flipped on the sound but left the image

blind. He barked, "Cancel battle stations order. It was an error."

The man at the other end spluttered something, and Devoure said sharply, "There's nothing wrong with the image. Get on the ball. Everyone back on routine." But almost against his will his hand hovered between his face and the place where the image ought to be, as though he feared that somehow the other might penetrate to vision anyhow and see to what his face had been reduced— and wonder about it.

Yonge's nostrils flared as he watched, and he slowly rubbed his scarred forearm.

Devoure sat down. "The rest of you stand," he said, and stared sullenly from face to face. "This Martian will die, maybe not by robot or in a stripped space ship. I'll think of something; and if you think you saved him, Earthman, be sure I'll think of something more amusing still. I have an excellent imagination."

Lucky said, "I demand that he be treated as a prisoner of war."

Devoure said, "There is no war. He is a spy. He deserves death. He is a roboticide. He deserves death twice." His voice trembled suddenly. "He lifted his hands against me. He deserves death a dozen times."

"I'll buy my friend," said Lucky in a whisper.

"He is not for sale."

"I can pay a high price."

"How?" Devoure grinned ferociously. "By bearing witness at the conference as you have been requested? It is too late for that. It is not enough."

"I couldn't do that in any case," said Lucky. "I

will not lie against Earth, but there is a truth I can tell; a truth you do not know."

Bigman said sharply, "Don't bargain with him, Lucky."

"The monkey is right," Devoure said. "Don't bargain. Nothing you can tell me will buy him. I wouldn't sell him for all Earth in my hand."

Yonge interrupted sharply, "I would for much less. Listen to the Councilman. Their lives may be worth the information they have."

Devoure said, "Don't provoke me. You are under arrest."

But Yonge lifted a chair and let it drop with a crash. "I defy you to arrest me. I'm a Serviceman. You can't execute me out of hand. You dare not, no matter how I provoke you. You must reserve me for trial. And at any trial I have things to say."

"Such as?" demanded Devoure with contempt.

All the dislike of the aging Serviceman for the young aristocrat was suddenly out in the open. "Such as what happened today: how a five-foot Terrestrial tore you apart until you howled and Zayon had to step in to save your life. Zayon will bear witness. Every man jack at the base will remember that you dared not show your face for days after this date—or will you have the nerve to show that torn face before it heals?"

"Be quiet!"

"I can be quiet. I need say nothing—if you will stop subordinating the good of Sirius to your private hatreds. Listen to what the Councilman has to say." He turned to Lucky. "I guarantee you a fair deal."

Bigman piped up, "What fair deal? You and Zayon will wake up one morning and find yourselves dead by accident and Devoure will be so sorry and send you lots of flowers, only after that there'll be no one to say how he needs robots to hide behind when a Martian is after his filthy skin. Then we'll go any way he likes. So why bargain?"

"There'll be nothing like that," said Yonge stiffly, "because I will give the complete story to one of the robots within an hour of my leaving here. He won't know which one, and he won't find out. If either Zayon or myself dies of anything but natural causes, the story will be relayed to the public sub-etherics in full; otherwise, not. I rather think Devoure will be anxious to see that nothing happens to Zayon or myself."

Zayon shook his head. "I don't like this, Yonge."

"You've got to like it, Zayon. You witnessed his beating. Do you think he wouldn't do his worst for you if you didn't take precautions? Come, I'm weary of sacrificing the honor of the Service to the nephew of the director."

Zayon said unhappily, "Well, what is your information, Councilman Starr?"

Lucky said in a low voice, "It's more than information. It's surrender. There is another Councilman on what you call Sirian territory. Agree to treat my friend as a prisoner of war and safeguard his life by forgetting the roboticide incident and I'll take you to this other Councilman."

13

Prelude to Vesta

Bigman, who, to the end, had been certain that Lucky had some stratagem on hand, was appalled. He called out in a heartbroken wail, "No, Lucky! No! I don't want to be pulled out that way."

Devoure was openly astonished. "Where? No ship could have penetrated our defenses. It's a lie."

"I'll take you to the man," said Lucky wearily, "if we come to an arrangement."

"Space!" growled Yonge. "It's an arrangement."

"Wait," said Devoure angrily. "I admit this could be of value to us, but is Starr suggesting that he will openly testify to the conference on Vesta that this other Councilman invaded our territory and that Starr voluntarily revealed his hiding place?"

"It's the truth," said Lucky. "I will so testify."

"The word of honor of a Councilman?" sneered Devoure.

"I have said I will testify."

"Well, then," said Devoure, "since our Servicemen *will* have it so, you may have your lives in exchange." His eyes suddenly sparked fury. "On Mimas. Is that it, Councilman? Mimas?"

"That is correct."

"By Sirius!" Devoure rose to his feet in agitation. "We almost missed it. Nor did this occur to the Service."

Zayon said with thought, "Mimas?"

"The Service still doesn't get it," said Devoure with a malignant scowl. "Three men were on *The Shooting Starr,* obviously. Three entered Mimas; two left; one stayed behind. It was your report, Yonge, I believe, which stressed the fact that Starr always worked with his companion in a party of two."

"He always had," said Yonge.

"And was there no flexibility left in you to consider the possibility of a third? Shall we go then to Mimas?" Devoure seemed to have lost his mad passion for revenge in the stress of this new development, almost to have regained the mocking irony he had displayed when the two Terrestrials had first landed on Titan. "And you will give us the pleasure of your company, Councilman?"

"Certainly, Mr. Devoure," said Lucky.

Bigman moved away, face averted. He felt worse now, he thought, than even in that last moment of robotic advance when the metal limbs were on his arm, ready to smash.

The Shooting Starr was in space again, but not as an independent ship. It was caught in firm magnetic grapple and moved according to the impulses of the engines of the accompanying Sirian ship.

The trip from Titan to Mimas took the better part of two days, and it was a hard time for Lucky, a bitter, suspenseful time.

He missed Bigman, who had been taken from him

and placed on the Sirian ship. (The two on separate ships, Devoure had pointed out, were hostages for each other's good behavior.)

It was the Sirian Serviceman, Harrig Zayon, who made the second on the ship. There was a stiffness about him. He made no effort to repeat his original attempt to convert Lucky Starr to Sirian views, and Lucky could not resist taking the offensive in the matter. He asked if Devoure were an example, in Zayon's eyes, of the superior race of human beings that inhabited the Sirian planets.

Zayon said reluctantly, "Devoure has not had the benefit of Service training and Service discipline. He is emotional."

"Your colleague, Yonge, seems to consider it more than that. He makes no secret of his low opinion of Devoure."

"Yonge is—is a representative of an extreme view among the Servicemen. That scar on his arm was received during some internal troubles that attended the rise of the present director of the Central Body to power."

"Devoure's uncle?"

"Yes. The Service was on the side of the previous director, and Yonge followed orders with Serviceman's honor. As a result he was passed over for promotion under the new regime. Oh, they send him out here and appoint him to the committee which will represent Sirius at Vesta, but in actual fact he is under Devoure."

"The director's nephew."

"Yes. And Yonge resents it. Yonge cannot bring himself to understand that the Service is an organ of the state and does not question its policies or have anything to do with the question of which individual or group is to govern it. He is an excellent Serviceman, otherwise."

"But you have not answered the question as to whether you found Devoure a satisfactory representative of the Sirian elite."

Zayon said angrily, "What about your Earth? Have you never had unsatisfactory rulers? Or even vicious ones?"

"Any number," admitted Lucky, "but we are a miscellaneous lot on Earth; we vary. No ruler can stay in power very long if he doesn't represent a compromise among us. Compromising rulers may not be dynamic, but neither are they tyrannical. On Sirius you have developed a sameness among yourselves, and a ruler can go to extremes along the lines of that sameness. For that reason autocracy and force in politics are not the exceptional interlude that they are on Earth, but are the rule with you."

Zayon sighed, but it was long hours before he spoke to Lucky again. It was not until Mimas was large in the visiplate and they were decelerating to land.

Zayon said, "Tell me, Councilman. I ask you on your honor. Is this a trick of some sort?"

Lucky's stomach tightened, but he said calmly, "What do you mean by a trick?"

"Is there really a Councilman on Mimas?"

"Yes, there is. What do you expect? That I have a force knot concealed on Mimas designed to blow us all to nothingness?"

"Perhaps something like that."

"And what would I gain? The destruction of one Sirian ship and a dozen Sirians?"

"You would gain your honor."

Lucky shrugged. "I have made a bargain. We have a Councilman down there. I will go and get him and there will be no resistance."

Zayon nodded. "Very well. I suppose you would not make a Sirian after all. You had better stay an Earthman."

Lucky smiled bitterly. That, then, was the source of Zayon's ill humor. His stiff Serviceman's sense of honor objected to Lucky's behavior even when he believed Sirius to be benefiting by it.

Back at Port Center, International City, Earth, Chief Councilman Hector Conway waited to leave for Vesta. He had not heard directly from Lucky since *The Shooting Starr* had moved into the shadow of Hidalgo.

The capsule brought in by Captain Bernold had been specific enough in its curt way and had been marked by Lucky's usual hard common sense. A call for a conference *had* been the only way out. The President had seen that at once, and though some members of the cabinet were bellicose about matters, they had been overruled.

Even Sirius (quite as Lucky had predicted) had adopted the notion eagerly. It was, obviously, exactly what the Sirian government wanted, a conference that was sure to fail, followed by a war on their own terms. To all outward appearances, they had all the cards.

It was that very fact that had made it so necessary

to keep as much as possible from the public. If all details were put on the sub-ether without careful preparation, an indignant public might howl Earth's government irresistibly into war against all the Galaxy. The call for a conference would only make matters worse, since it would be interpreted as a cowardly sell-out to the Sirians.

And yet complete secrecy was impossible, too, and the press was angry and rebellious at being fed diluted government reports. Things were worsening daily.

The President would have to hold out somehow until the conference could take place. And yet, if the conference failed, the present situation would be honey-sweet compared to that which would come.

In the general indignation that would follow, there would be not only war, but the Council of Science would be completely discredited and destroyed, and the Terrestrial Federation would lose its most powerful weapon just when it needed it most.

It had been weeks since Hector Conway had slept without pills, and for the first time in his career he thought earnestly that he should be retiring.

He rose heavily and made his way forward to the ship now being readied for the launching. In a week he would be on Vesta for preliminary discussions with Doremo. That old pink-eyed statesman would be holding the balance of power. There was no doubting that. The very weakness of his small world was what made him powerful. He was the nearest thing to an honest and disinterested neutral in the Galaxy, and even the Sirians would listen to him.

If Conway could get his ear to begin with . . .

He was scarcely aware of the man approaching to stop him until there was a near collision.

"Eh? What is this?" demanded Conway in annoyance.

The man touched the brim of his hat. "Jan Dieppe of Trans-sub-etheric, Chief. I wonder if you would answer a few questions?"

"No, no. I'm ready to board ship."

"I realize that, sir. It's the very reason I'm stopping you. I won't get another chance. You're heading out for Vesta, of course."

"Yes, of course."

"To see about the outrage on Saturn."

"Well?"

"What do you expect the conference to do, Chief? Do you suppose Sirius will listen to resolutions and votes?"

"Yes, I think Sirius will."

"Do you think the votes will go against her?"

"I'm sure they will. Now may I pass?"

"I'm sorry, sir, but there's something very important just now that Earth's people must know about."

"Please. Don't tell me what you think they must know. I assure you that the good of Earth's people is close to my heart."

"And is that why the Council of Science is willing to allow foreign governments to vote on whether or not the Terrestrial Federation's territory has been invaded? A question that should be reserved to our own decision alone?"

Conway could not fail to note the undercurrent of threat in the other's outwardly polite but persistent questioning. He looked over the reporter's shoulder

and could see the Secretary of State talking to a group
of other newsmen at a point closer to the ship.

He said, "What are you getting at?"

"The public is questioning the good faith of the
Council, I'm afraid, Chief. And in that connection,
Trans-sub-ether has picked up a Sirian news broadcast that it has not yet made public. We need your
comments on it."

"No comments. A Sirian news broadcast designed
for home consumption is not worth comment."

"This report was quite circumstantial. For instance,
where is Councilman David Starr, the legendary Lucky,
himself? Where is he?"

"What?"

"Come on now, Chief. I know the Council's agents
dislike publicity, but has Councilman Starr been sent
to Saturn on a secret mission?"

"Now if that were so, young man, would you expect
me to talk about it?"

"Yes, if Sirius were already talking about it. It's no
secret to them. They say Lucky Starr invaded the Saturnian system and was captured. Is that true?"

Conway said stiffly, "I do not know the present
whereabouts of Councilman David Starr."

"Does that mean he *might* be in the Saturnian system?"

"It means that I do not know his whereabouts."

The reporter's nose wrinkled. "All right. If you
think it sounds better to have the Chief of the Council
of Science deny that he knows the whereabouts of one
of his important agents, that's your business. But the
general mood of the public is increasingly anti-
Council. There is considerable talk of the Council's

inefficiency in letting Sirius get to Saturn in the first place and its interest in whitewashing the whole affair for the sake of their political skins."

"You are being insulting. Good day, sir."

"The Sirians are quite definite that Lucky Starr has been captured in the Saturnian system. Any comment on that?"

"No. Let me pass."

"The Sirians say that Lucky Starr will be at the conference."

"Oh?" For a moment Conway could not conceal a spasm of interest.

"That seems to get you, Chief. The only catch is that the Sirians say he'll be testifying for *them*."

Conway said with difficulty, "That remains to be seen."

"Do you admit he'll be at the conference?"

"I know nothing about that."

The reporter stepped aside. "All right, Chief. It's just that the Sirians say that Starr has already given them valuable information and that the Sirians will be able to convict us of aggression on the basis of it. I mean, what's the Council doing? Fighting with us or against us?"

Conway, feeling unbearably harried, muttered, "No comment," and started to pass by.

The reporter called after him. "Starr is your adopted son, isn't he, Chief?"

For a moment Conway turned back. Then, without a word, he hastened on to the ship.

What was there to say? What *could* he say except that ahead of him lay an interstellar conference more crucial for Earth than any meeting of any sort in its history? That this conference was weighted heavily on the side of Sirius. That chances were almost intolerably great that peace, the Council of Science, the Terrestrial Federation would all be destroyed.

And that only the thin shield of Lucky's efforts protected them.

Somehow, what depressed Conway more than anything else—more, even, than a lost war—was the thought that if the Sirian news report were true and if the conference nevertheless failed despite Lucky's original intentions, Lucky would go down in history as Earth's arch-traitor! And only a few would ever know better.

14

On Vesta

The Secretary of State, Lamont Finney, was a career politician who had served some fifteen years in the legislature and whose relations with the Council of Science had never been overwhelmingly friendly. He was aging now, not in the best of health, and inclined to be querulous. Officially he headed the Terrestrial delegation to Vesta. In actuality, though, Conway understood quite well that he, himself, as head of the Council, must be prepared to take full responsibility for failure—if there was failure.

Finney made that clear even before the ship, one of Earth's largest space liners, took off.

He said, "The press is almost uncontrollable. You're in a bad spot, Conway."

"All Earth is."

"*You*, Conway."

Conway said gloomily, "Well, I am under no illusions that if things go badly the Council can expect support from the government."

"I'm afraid not." The Secretary of State was strapping himself in with meticulous care against the rigors of take-off and making certain that his bottle of anti-space-sickness pills were handy. "Government support for you would only mean the downfall of the government, and there will be enough troubles with a war emergency. We can't afford political instability."

Conway thought: He has no confidence in the outcome of the conference at all. He expects the war.

He said, "Listen, Finney, if the worst does come to the worst, I will need voices on my side to help prevent Councilman Starr's reputation from———"

Finney lifted his gray head momentarily from the hydraulic cushion and stared at the other out of fading, troubled eyes. "Impossible. Your Councilman went into Saturn on his own, asked no permission, received no orders. He was willing to take the risks. If things turn out badly, he is done. What else can we do?"

"You *know* he———"

"I *don't* know," said the politician violently. "I know nothing officially. You've been in public life long enough to know that under certain conditions the people need a scapegoat and insist on one. Councilman Starr will be the scapegoat."

He leaned back again, closed his eyes, and Conway leaned back beside him. Elsewhere in the ship others were in their places, and the far thunder of the engines started up and rose in pitch as the ship raised itself slowly from the launching pad and lifted toward the sky.

The Shooting Starr hovered a thousand miles above Vesta, caught in its feeble gravity and circling it slowly with engines blocked. Grappled to it was a small lifeboat from the Sirian mother ship.

Serviceman Zayon had left *The Shooting Starr* to join the Sirian delegation on Vesta, and a robot remained behind in his place. In the lifeboat was Bigman, and with him Serviceman Yonge.

Lucky had been surprised when Yonge's face first stared out at him in the receiver. He said, "What are you doing out in space? Is Bigman with you?"

"He is. I'm his guard. I suppose you expected a robot."

"Yes, I did. Or won't they trust Bigman with a robot after last time?"

"No, this is just Devoure's little way of seeing to it that I don't attend the conference. It's a slap at the Service."

Lucky said, "Serviceman Zayon will be there."

"Zayon," Yonge sniffed. "He is an adequate man, but he's a follower. He can't realize that there's more to the Service than blindly obeying orders from above; that we owe it to Sirius to see to it that she is ruled according to the inflexible principles of honor that guide the Service itself."

Lucky said, "How is Bigman?"

"Well enough. He seems unhappy. It's strange that such an odd-looking person should have a sterner sense of duty and honor than a person like yourself."

Lucky clamped his lips together. There was little time left, and it worried him whenever either Serviceman began speculating about Lucky's loss of honor. From that it was a step to wondering if Lucky might by some chance have retained his honor, and then they might wonder what his intentions really were, and after that——

Yonge shrugged. "Well, I called only to make sure all was well. I am responsible for your welfare until, in good time, we get you down before the conference."

"Wait, Serviceman. You performed a service for me back on Titan————"

"I did nothing for you. I followed the dictates of duty."

"Nevertheless, you saved Bigman's life and mine, too, perhaps. It may so happen that when the conference is over you may consider your life in danger."

"*My* life?"

Lucky said carefully, "Once I have given evidence, Devoure may for one reason or another decide to get rid of you despite the risk of having Sirians find out about his fight with Bigman."

Yonge laughed bitterly. "He wasn't seen once on the trip out here. He was waiting in his cabin for his face to heal. I'm safe enough."

"Just the same, if you consider yourself in danger, approach Hector Conway, Chief Councilman of Science. My word on it that he will accept you as a political exile."

"I suppose you mean that kindly," said Yonge, "but I think that after the conference it will be Conway who will have to seek political asylum." Yonge broke connections.

And Lucky was left to look down at gleaming Vesta and to think sadly that, after all, the chances were heavily in favor of Yonge's being right.

Vesta was one of the largest of the asteroids. It was not the size of Ceres, which was more than five hundred miles in diameter and a giant among asteroids, but its 215-mile span put it into the second class, where only two other asteroids, Pallas and Juno, competed with it.

As seen from Earth, Vesta was the brightest of the asteroids because of the chance that had composed its outermost shell so largely of calcium carbonate rather than the darker silicates and metallic oxides that made up the other asteroids.

Scientists speculated on this odd divergence in chemical constitution (which had not been suspected until an actual landing was made upon it; before that the ancient astronomers had wondered if Vesta lay under a coat of ice or frozen carbon dioxide) but had come to no conclusion. And the feature writers took to calling it the "world of marble."

The "world of marble" had been converted into a naval base in the first days of the fight with the space pirates of the asteroid belt. The natural caverns under its surface had been enlarged and made airtight, and there had been room to store a fleet and house two years of provisions for it.

Now the naval base was more or less obsolete, but with small changes the caverns could be (and had been) made a most suitable meeting ground for delegates from all over the Galaxy.

Food and water supplies had been laid down, and luxuries which naval men had not required were added. As one passed the marble surface and entered the interior, there was little to distinguish Vesta from an Earthside hotel.

The Terrestrial delegation as the hosts (Vesta was Terrestrial territory; not even the Sirians could dispute that) assigned the quarters and saw to it that the delegates were comfortable. This meant the adjustment of the various quarters to the slight difference in gravity and atmospheric conditions to which the delegates might be accustomed. Those from Warren, for instance, had the quarters air-conditioned to a moderate chill to allow for the frigid climate of their home planet.

It was not an accident that greatest pains were taken for the delegation from Elam. It was a small world circling a red dwarf star. Its environment was such that one would not have supposed human beings could flourish there. Yet the very deficiencies were turned into account by the restless ingenuity of the human species.

There was not enough light to allow Earth-type plants to grow properly, so artificial lights were used and special breeds were cultivated, until Elamite grains and agricultural products generally were not merely adequate but of superior quality that could not be duplicated elsewhere in the Galaxy. Elamite prosperity rested on her agricultural exports in a way that other worlds more favored by nature could not match.

Probably as a result of the poor light of Elam's sun, there was no biological favoring of skin pigmentation. The inhabitants were fair-skinned almost to extremes.

The head of the Elamite delegation, for instance, was almost an albino. He was Agas Doremo, for more than thirty years the recognized leader of the neutralist forces in the Galaxy. In every question that arose between Earth and Sirius (which, of course, represented the extreme anti-Terrestrial forces of the Galaxy) he held the balance even.

Conway counted on him to do so in this case too. He entered the quarters assigned to the Elamite with an air of friendship. He took care to keep from being overeffusive and shook hands warmly. He blinked in the low-pitched, red-tinged light and accepted a glass of native Elamite brew.

Doremo said, "Your hair has grown white since last I saw you, Conway—as white as mine."

"It has been many years since we last met, Doremo."

"Then it hasn't grown white just these last few months?"

Conway smiled ruefully. "It would have, I think, if it had been dark to begin with."

Doremo nodded and sipped his drink. He said, "Earth has let itself be placed in a most uncomfortable position."

"So it has, and yet by all the rules of logic, Earth is in the right."

"Yes?" Doremo was noncommittal.

"I don't know how much thought you've given this matter——"

"Considerable."

"Or how willing you are to discuss the matter in advance——"

"Why not? The Sirians have been at me."

"Ah. Already?"

"I stopped off at Titan on the way in." Doremo shook his head. "They've got a beautiful base there, as I could see once they supplied me with dark glasses— it's the horrible blue light of Sirius that spoils things, of course. You have to give them credit, Conway; they do things with a splash."

"Have you decided that they have a right to colonize Saturn?"

Doremo said, "My dear Conway, I have decided only that I want peace. A war will do no one any good. The situation, however, is this: The Sirians are in the

Saturnian system. How can they be forced out of it without war?"

"There is one way," said Conway. "If the other outer worlds were to make it clear that they considered Sirius to be an invader, Sirius could not face the enmity of all the Galaxy."

"Ah, but how are the outer worlds to be persuaded to vote against Sirius?" Doremo said. "Most of them, if you'll forgive me, have a traditional suspicion of Earth, and they will tell themselves that the Saturnian system was, after all, uninhabited."

"But it has been a settled assumption since Earth first granted independence to the outer worlds, as a result of the Hegellian Doctrine, that no smaller unit than a stellar system is to be considered capable of independence. An unoccupied planetary system means nothing unless the stellar system of which it is a part is unoccupied as a whole."

"I agree with you. I admit that this has been the assumption. However, the assumption has never been put to the test. Now it will be."

"Do you think," said Conway softly, "that it would be wise to destroy the assumption, to accept a new principle that would allow any stranger to enter a system and colonize such unpopulated planets or planetoids as he may come across?"

"No," said Doremo emphatically, "I do *not* think so. I think it to the best interests of all of us that stellar systems continue to be considered as indivisible, but——"

"But?"

"There will be passions aroused at this conference that will make it difficult for delegates to approach matters logically. If I may presume to advise Earth——"

"Go ahead. This is unofficial and off the record."

"I would say, count on no support at this conference. Allow Sirius to remain on Saturn for the present. She will overplay her hand eventually and then you can call a second conference with higher hopes."

Conway shook his head. "Impossible. If we fail here, there will be passions aroused on our side; they are aroused already."

Doremo shrugged. "Passions everywhere. I am very pessimistic about this."

Conway said persuasively, "But if you yourself believe that Sirius ought not to be on Saturn, could you not make an effort to persuade others of this? You are a person of influence who commands the respect of the Galaxy. I don't ask you to do anything but stick by your own belief. It may make all the difference between war and peace."

Doremo put his glass aside and dabbed at his lip with a napkin. "It is what I would very much like to do, Conway, but I don't even dare to try at this conference. Sirius has matters so entirely its own way that it might be dangerous for Elam to stand against them. We are a small world. . . . After all, Conway, if you called this conference in order to reach a peaceful solution, why did you simultaneously send war vessels into the Saturnian system?"

"Is that what the Sirians told you, Doremo?"

"Yes. They showed me some of the evidence they had. I was even shown a captured Earth ship in flight to Vesta under the magnetic grapple of a Sirian vessel. I was told that no less a person than Lucky Starr, of whom even we on Elam have heard somewhat, was on board. I understand Starr is circling off Vesta now, waiting to testify."

Slowly Conway nodded.

Doremo said, "Now if Starr admits to warlike actions against the Sirians—and he will, otherwise it is inconceivable the Sirians will allow him to testify—then it will be all the conference needs. No arguments will stand against it. Starr, I believe, is an adopted son of yours."

"In a way, yes," muttered Conway.

"That makes it worse, you see. And if you say that he acted without Earth's sanction, as I suppose you must——"

"It's true that he did," said Conway, "but I am not prepared to say what we will claim."

"If you disown him, no one will believe you. Your own son, you see. The outer-world delegates will set up the cry of 'perfidious Terrestria,' of Earth's supposed hypocrisy. Sirius will make the most of it, and I'll be able to do nothing. I will not even be able to cast my personal vote in favor of Earth. . . . Earth had better give in now."

Conway shook his head. "Earth cannot."

"Then," said Doremo with infinite sadness, "it will mean war, with all of us against Earth, Conway."

15

The Conference

Conway had finished his drink. Now he rose to go, shaking hands with a look of settled melancholy on his face.

He said, almost as an afterthought, "But you know, we haven't heard Lucky's testimony yet. If the effects aren't as bad as you think, if his testimony should even prove harmless, would you work then on behalf of peace?"

Doremo shrugged. "You are grasping at straws. Yes, yes, in the unlikely case that the conference is not stampeded past recall by your foster son's words, I will do my bit. As I told you, I am really on your side."

"I thank you, sir." They shook hands again.

Doremo stared after the departing Chief Councilman with a sad little shake of his head. Outside the door, however, Conway paused to catch his breath. It was really quite as much as he had expected. Now if only the Sirians *would* present Lucky.

The conference opened on the stiff and formal note to be expected. Everyone was painfully correct, and when Earth's delegation entered to take their posts in the front and at the extreme right of the hall, all the delegates already seated, even the Sirians in the front and extreme left, rose.

When the Secretary of State, representing the host power, rose to make a welcoming speech, he spoke in generalities about peace and the door it opened to the continuing expansion of mankind through the Galaxy, of the common ancestry and brotherhood of all men, of the grievous disaster war would be. He carefully made no mention of the specific points of issue, did not refer to Sirius by name, and, above all, made no threats.

He was graciously applauded. Then the conference voted Agas Doremo into the chair to preside (he was the only man on whom both sides could agree), and the chief business of the conference began.

The conference was not open to the public, but there were special booths for reporters from the various worlds represented. They were not to interview individual delegates but were allowed to listen and send out uncensored reports.

The proceedings, as was customary in such interstellar gatherings, were carried on in Interlingua, the language amalgam that served throughout the Galaxy.

After a short speech by Doremo extolling the virtues of compromise and begging no one to be so stubborn as to risk war where a slight yielding might insure peace, he recognized Earth's Secretary of State once more.

This time the Secretary was a partisan, presenting his side of the dispute forcefully and well.

There was, however, no mistaking the hostile attitude of the other delegates. It hung like a fog over the assembly hall.

Conway sat next to the orating Secretary, with his chin digging into his chest. Ordinarily it would be a mistake for Earth to present its major speech at the very start. It would be a case of shooting off the best ammunition before the nature of the target was known. It would give Sirius the opportunity for a crushing rebuttal.

But in this case, however, this was exactly what Conway wanted.

He whipped out a handkerchief, passed it over his forehead, then put it hastily back and hoped he had not been noticed. He did not want to seem worried.

Sirius reserved its rebuttal and, undoubtedly by arrangement, representatives of three of the outer worlds, three that were notoriously under Sirian influence, rose to speak briefly. Each avoided the direct problem but commented forcefully on the aggressive intentions of Earth and on its ambitions to reimpose a galactic government under its own rule. They set the stage for the eventual Sirian display and, having done so, there was a lunch recess.

Finally, six hours after the conference had been called to order, Sten Devoure of Sirius was recognized and rose slowly to his feet. He stepped forward with quiet deliberation to the rostrum and stood there, looking down upon the delegates with an expression of proud confidence on his olive-skinned face. (There was no sign of his misadventure with Bigman.)

There was a stir among the delegates that quieted

only after a number of minutes during which Devoure made no effort to begin speaking.

Conway was certain that every delegate knew that Lucky Starr would be testifying soon. They were waiting for this complete humiliation of Earth with excitement and anticipation.

Devoure began his speech at last, very quietly. His introduction was historical. Going back to the days when Sirius was a Terrestrial colony, he rehearsed once again the grievances of that day. He brushed over the Hegellian Doctrine, which had established the independence of Sirius as well as that of the other colonies, as insincere, and one by one cited the supposed efforts of Earth to re-establish domination.

Coming down to the present, he said, "We are now accused of having colonized an unoccupied world. We plead guilty to that. We are accused of having taken an empty world and made it a beautiful habitation for human beings. We plead guilty to that. We are accused of extending the range of the human race to a world suitable for it that had been neglected by others. We plead guilty to that.

"We have not been accused of offering violence to anyone in the process. We have not been accused of making war, of killing and wounding, in the course of our occupation. We are accused of no crime at all. Instead, it is merely stated that not quite a billion miles away from the world we now so peacefully occupy there is another occupied world named Earth.

"We are not aware that this has anything to do with our world, Saturn. We offer no violence to Earth, and they accuse us of none. We ask only the privilege of being left to ourselves, and in return for that we are glad to offer to leave them to themselves.

"They say Saturn is theirs. Why? Have they occupied its satellites at any time? No. Have they shown interest in it? No. For the thousands of years during which it was theirs for the taking, did they want it? No. It was only after we landed on it that they suddenly discovered their interest in it.

"They say Saturn circles about the same Sun that Earth does. We admit that, but we also point out that the fact is irrelevant. An empty world is an empty world, regardless of the particular route it travels through space. We colonized it first and it is ours.

"Now I have said that Sirius occupied the Saturnian system without force of any kind and without the threat of force; that we are actuated in all we do by a desire for peace. We do not speak much of peace, as Earth does, but we at least practice it. When Earth called for a conference, we accepted at once, for the sake of peace, even though there is no shadow of any sort on our title to the Saturnian system.

"But what of Earth? How does it back *its* views? They are very fluent in their talks on peace, but their actions match their words very poorly. They called for peace and practiced war. They demanded a conference and at the same time outfitted a war expedition. In short, while Sirius risked its interests for the sake of peace, Earth, in return, made unprovoked war upon us. I can prove this from the mouth of a member of Earth's own Council of Science."

He raised his hand as he spoke the last sentence, his first gesture of any sort, and pointed dramatically to a doorway upon which a spot of light had been allowed to fall. Lucky Starr was standing there, tall and defiantly straight. A robot flanked him on either side.

Lucky, on being brought down to Vesta, finally saw Bigman again. The little Martian ran to him, while Yonge looked on with dour amusement from a distance.

"Lucky," pleaded Bigman. "Sands of Mars, Lucky, don't go through with it. They can't make you say a word if you don't want to, and it doesn't really matter what happens to me."

Slowly Lucky shook his head. "Wait, Bigman. Wait one more day."

Yonge came up and took Bigman by the elbow. "Sorry, Starr, but we need him till you're through. Devoure has a great sense of hostage, and at this point I rather think he's right. You're going to have to face your own people, and dishonor will be difficult."

Lucky nerved himself for just that when he finally stood in the doorway and felt the eyes upon him, the silence, the caught breaths. In the spotlight himself, Lucky saw the delegates to the conference as nothing but a giant black mass. It was only after the robots led him into the witness box that faces swam out of the crowd at him, and he could see Hector Conway in the front row.

For a moment Conway smiled at him with weary affection, but Lucky dared not smile back. This was the crisis and he must do nothing that, even at this late moment, might warn the Sirians.

Devoure stared at the Earthman hungrily, savoring

his coming triumph. He said, "Gentlemen. I wish temporarily to convert this conference into something approaching a court of law. I have a witness here whom I wish all the delegates to hear. I well rest my case on what he says—he, an Earthman and an important agent of the Council of Science."

He then said to Lucky with sudden sharpness, "Your name, citizenship, and position, please."

Lucky said, "I am David Starr, native of Earth, and member of the Council of Science."

"Have you been subjected to drugs, to psychic probing, or to mental violence of any sort to induce you to testify here?"

"No, sir."

"You speak voluntarily, and will tell the truth?"

"I speak voluntarily and will tell the truth."

Devoure turned to the delegates. "It may occur to some of you that Councilman Starr has indeed been handled mentally without his knowledge or that he may be denying mental harm as the very result of that mental harm. If so, he may be examined by any member of this conference with medical qualification—I know there are a number of such—if anyone demands such examination."

No one made the demand, and Devoure went on, addressing Lucky, "When did you first become aware of the Sirian base within the Saturnian system?"

Curtly, unemotionally, eyes staring stonily forward, Lucky told of the first entry into the Saturnian system and the warning to leave.

Conway nodded slightly at Lucky's complete omission of the capsule or of Agent X's spying activities. Agent X might have been merely a Terrestrial criminal. Obviously Sirius wanted no mention of its own spying at this time and, as obviously, Lucky was satisfied to go along with them in this.

"And did you leave after being warned?"

"I did, sir."

"Permanently?"

"No, sir."

"What did you do next?"

Lucky described the ruse with Hidalgo, the approach to Saturn's south pole, the flight through the gap in the rings to Mimas.

Devoure interrupted, "Did we at any time offer violence to your ship?"

"No, sir."

Devoure turned to the delegates again. "There is no need to rely only upon the word of the Councilman. I have here telephotos of the pursuit of the Councilman's ship to Mimas."

While Lucky remained in the spotlight the rest of the chamber was darkened, and in the three-dimensional imagery the delegates watched scenes of *The Shooting Starr* speeding toward the rings and disappearing into a gap which, at the angle of photography, could not be seen.

It was next shown racing headlong into Mimas and disappearing in a flash of ruddy light and vapor.

At this time Devoure must have felt the growth of a furtive admiration for the daring of the Earthman, for he said with a touch of annoyed haste, "Our inability to overtake the Councilman was the result of his ship's equipment with Agrav motors. Maneuvers in the neighborhood of Saturn were more difficult for us than for him. For that reason we ourselves had not previously approached Mimas and were not psychologically ready for his doing so."

If Conway had dared he would have shouted aloud at that. The fool! Devoure would pay for that moment of jealousy. Of course by mentioning Agrav he was trying to stir up the outer worlds' fears of Earth's scientific advances, and that might be a mistake too. The fears might grow too strong.

Devoure said to Lucky, "Now then, what happened once you left Mimas?"

Lucky described his capture, and Devoure, having hinted at Sirius's possession of advanced mass-detection devices, said, "And then, once on Titan, did you give us further information concerning your activities on Mimas?"

"Yes, sir. I told you that another Councilman was still on Mimas, and then I accompanied you back to Mimas."

This the delegates had apparently not known. There was a furor, which Devoure shouted down. He cried, "I have a complete telephoto of the removal of the Councilman from Mimas, where he was sent to establish a secret war base against us at the very time that Earth called this conference, allegedly for peace."

Again the darkening and again the three-dimensional image. In full detail the conference watched the landing on Mimas, saw the surface melted down, watched Lucky disappear into the tunnel formed and Councilman Ben Wessilewsky brought up and on board ship. The last scenes were those taken within Wess's temporary quarters under the surface of Mimas.

"A fully equipped base, as you see," said Devoure. Then, turning to Lucky, he said, "May your actions throughout all this be considered to have the official approval of Earth?"

It was a leading question and there was no doubt as to the answer that was desired and expected, but here Lucky hesitated, while the audience waited breathlessly and a frown gathered on Devoure's face.

Finally Lucky said, "I will tell the precise truth. I did not receive direct permission to re-enter Saturn a second time, but I know that in everything I did I would have met with the full approval of the Council of Science."

And at that admission there was wild commotion among the reporters and a hubbub on the floor. The conference delegates were rising in their seats, and cries of "Vote! Vote!" could be made out.

To all appearances the conference had ended and Earth had lost.

16

Biter Bit

Agas Doremo was on his feet, banging the traditional gavel for silence with complete ineffectuality. Conway plowed forward through a host of threatening gestures and catcalls and pulled the circuit breaker, thus sounding the old pirate warning. A shrill rising-falling rasp of sound squealed above the disorder and beat the delegates into surprised silence.

Conway shut it off, and in the sudden quiet Doremo said quickly, "I have agreed to recognize Chief Councilman Hector Conway of the Terrestrial Federation that he might cross-examine Councilman Starr."

There were shouts of "No, no," but Doremo continued obdurately, "I ask the conference to play fair in this respect. The Chief Councilman assures me his cross-examination will be brief."

Amid rustling and a tide of whispering, Conway approached Lucky.

He smiled but spoke with an air of formality, saying, "Councilman Starr, Mr. Devoure did not question you as to your intentions in all this. Tell me, why did you enter the Saturnian system?"

"In order to colonize Mimas, Chief."

"Did you feel you had the right to do so?"

"It was an empty world, Chief."

Conway turned so as to face a suddenly puzzled and quiet group of delegates. "Would you repeat that, Councilman Starr?"

"I wished to establish human beings on Mimas, an empty world that belongs to the Terrestrial Federation, Chief."

Devoure was on his feet, calling out furiously, "Mimas is part of the Saturnian system."

"Exactly," said Lucky, "as Saturn is part of Earth's Solar System. But by *your* interpretation Mimas is merely an empty world. A while ago you admitted that Sirian ships had never approached Mimas before my ship landed on it."

Conway smiled. Lucky had caught that error on Devoure's part too.

Conway said, "Councilman Starr was not here, Mr. Devoure, when you made your introductory speech. Let me quote a passage from it, word for word: 'An empty world is an empty world, regardless of the particular route it travels through space. We colonized it first and it is ours.'"

The Chief Councilman turned toward the delegates and said with great deliberation, "If the viewpoint of the Terrestrial Federation is correct, then Mimas is Earth's, because it circles a planet that circles our Sun. If the viewpoint of Sirius is correct, then Mimas is still Earth's, because it was empty and we colonized it first. By Sirius's own line of reasoning, the fact that another satellite of Saturn was colonized by Sirius had nothing to do with the case.

"In either event, by invading a world belonging to the Terrestrial Federation and removing therefrom our colonist, Sirius has committed an act of war and has shown its true hypocrisy, since it refused to allow others the rights it claimed for itself."

And now again there was a confused milling about, and it was Doremo who spoke next. "Gentlemen, I have something to say. The facts, as stated by Councilmen Starr and Conway, are irrefutable. This demonstrates the complete anarchy into which the Galaxy would be thrown if the Sirian view were to prevail. Every uninhabited rock would be a source of contention, every asteroid a threat to peace. The Sirians, by their own action, have shown themselves insincere——"

It was a complete and sudden change-about.

Had time been allowed, Sirius might yet have rallied its forces, but Doremo, an experienced and skilled parliamentarian, maneuvered the conference into a vote while the pro-Sirians were still completely demoralized and before they had a chance to consider whether they dared go against the plain facts as suddenly revealed.

Three worlds voted on the side of Sirius. They were Penthesileia, Duvarn, and Mullen, all small and all known to be under Sirius's political influence. The rest of the Council, better than fifty votes, was on the side of Earth. Sirius was ordered to release the Earthmen it had taken prisoner. It was ordered to dismantle its base and leave the Solar System within a month.

The orders could not be enforced except by war, of course, but Earth was ready for war and Sirius would have to face it now without the help of the outer worlds. There wasn't a man on Vesta who expected her to fight under those conditions.

Devoure, panting and his face contorted, saw Lucky once more. "It was a foul trick," he said. "It was a device to force us into——"

"You forced *me,*" said Lucky quietly, "by the threat to Bigman's life. Do you remember? Or would you like the details of that published?"

"We still have your monkey friend," began Devoure malignantly, "and conference vote or not——"

Chief Councilman Conway, also present, smiled. "If you're referring to Bigman, Mr. Devoure, you don't have him. He is in our hands, together with a Serviceman named Yonge, who told me that Councilman Starr had assured him safe-conduct in case of need. He apparently feels that in your present mood it would be unsafe for himself to accompany you back to Titan. May I suggest that you consider whether it might be unsafe for you to go back to Sirius? If you wish to apply for asylum——"

But Devoure, speechless, turned his back and left.

Doremo was all a-grin as he bade farewell to Conway and Lucky.

"You'll be glad to see Earth again, I dare say, young man."

Lucky nodded his agreement. "I'm going home by liner within the hour, sir, with the poor old *Shooter* being towed along behind, and frankly, there's nothing that could please me more just now."

"Good! And congratulations on a magnificent piece of work. When Chief Conway asked me to allow him time for cross-examination at the beginning of the session, I agreed, but thought he must be mad. When you were done testifying and he signaled for recognition, I was *sure* he was mad. But obviously all this was planned in advance."

Conway said, "Lucky had sent me a message outlining what he hoped to do. Of course it wasn't till the last hour or two that we were sure it had worked out."

"I think you had faith in the Councilman," said Doremo. "Why, in your first conversation with me, you asked if I would come out on your side if Lucky's evidence failed of effect. I didn't see what you could mean then, of course, but I understood when the time came."

"I thank you for throwing your weight to our side."

"I threw it on the side of what had obviously been demonstrated to be justice. . . . You're a subtle opponent, young man," he said to Lucky.

Lucky smiled. "I merely counted on Sirius's lack of sincerity. If they had really believed in what they claimed was their point of view, my Councilman colleague would have been left on Mimas and all we would have had for our pains was a small satellite of ice and a difficult war to fight."

"Quite. Well, no doubt there'll be second thoughts when the delegates get back home, and some will become angry with Earth and with me and even with themselves, I suppose, for having let themselves be stampeded. In cold blood, though, they'll realize that they have established a principle here, the indivisibility of stellar systems, and I think they'll also realize that the good of this principle will outweigh any hurt to their pride or their prejudices. I really think this conference will be looked back on by historians as something important and as something that contributed a great deal to the peace and welfare of the Galaxy. I'm quite pleased."

And he shook hands with both, most vigorously.

Lucky and Bigman were together again, and though the ship was large and the passenger complement numerous, they kept to themselves. Mars was behind them (Bigman spending the better part of an hour observing it with great satisfaction) and Earth not very far ahead.

Bigman finally managed to voice his embarrassment. "Space, Lucky," he said, "I never saw what you were doing, not once. I thought—— Well, I don't want to say what I thought. Only, Sands of Mars, I wish you had warned me."

"Bigman, I couldn't. That was the one thing I couldn't do. Don't you see? I had to maneuver the Sirians into hijacking Wess off Mimas without letting them see the implications. I couldn't show them I *wanted* them to do it or they'd have seen the trap at once. I had to work it so that it would seem I was being forced into it bitterly against my will. At the start, I assure you, I didn't know exactly how I was going to do it, but I did know one thing—if *you* knew about the plan, Bigman, you'd have given the show away."

Bigman was outraged. "I'd give it away? Why, you Earthslug, a blaster couldn't have forced it out of me."

"I know. No torture could have forced it out of you, Bigman. You'd just give it away, free. You're a miserable actor and you know it. Once you got mad, it would come spilling out, one way or another. That's why I half wanted you to stay on Mimas, remember?

I knew I couldn't tell you the planned course of action and I knew you'd misunderstand what I was doing and be miserable about it. As it was, though, you turned out a godsend."

"I did? For beating up that cobber?"

"Indirectly, yes. It gave me the opportunity to make it look as though I were sincerely swapping Wess's freedom for your life. It took less acting to do that than to give Wess away under any conditions I could have dreamed up in your absence. In fact, as it was, I didn't have to act at all. It was a good swap."

"Aw, Lucky."

"Aw, yourself. Besides, you were so heartbroken about it that they never suspected a trick. Anyone watching you would have been convinced I was really betraying Earth."

"Sands of Mars, Lucky," said Bigman, stricken, "I should have known you wouldn't do anything like that. I was a nitwit."

"I'm glad you were," said Lucky fervently, and he ruffled the little fellow's hair affectionately.

When Conway and Wess joined them at dinner, Wess said, "This isn't going to be the kind of homecoming that fellow Devoure can expect. Ship's subether is full of the stuff they're printing on Earth about us; about you especially, of course."

Lucky frowned. "That's nothing to be thankful about. It just makes our job harder in the future. Publicity! Stop and think what they would be saying if the Sirians had been just one inch smarter and hadn't fallen for the bait or had pulled out of the conference at the last minute."

Conway shuddered visibly. "I'd rather not. But whatever it would be, that's what Devoure is getting."

Lucky said, "I guess he'll survive. His uncle will pull him through."

"Anyway," said Bigman, "we're through with him."

"Are we?" said Lucky somberly. "I wonder."

And they ate in silence for a few moments.

Conway, in an obvious attempt to alter the suddenly darkened atmosphere, said, "Of course, in a sense the Sirians could not afford to leave Wess on Mimas, so we didn't really give them a fair chance. After all, they were looking for the capsule in the rings, and for all they know, Wess, only thirty thousand miles outside the rings, might——"

Bigman dropped his fork, and his eyes were like saucers. *"Blasting rockets!"*

What's the matter, Bigman?" asked Wess kindly. "Did you accidentally think of something and sprain your brain?"

"Shut up, leather-head," said Bigman. "Listen, Lucky, in all this mess we forgot about Agent X's capsule. It's still out there in the rings unless the Sirians have found it already; and it they haven't, they still have a couple of weeks to do it in."

Conway said at once, "I've thought of that, Bigman. But frankly, I consider it lost for good. You can't find anything in the rings."

"But, Chief, hasn't Lucky told you about the special X-ray mass detectors they have and——"

By then, though, all were staring at Lucky. He had a queer look on his face, as though he couldn't make up his mind whether to laugh or to swear. "Great Galaxy," he cried. "I forgot about it completely."

"The capsule?" said Bigman. "You forgot it?"

"Yes. I forgot I had it. Here it is." And Lucky brought something metallic and about an inch in diameter out of his pocket and put it on the table.

Bigman's nimble fingers were on it first, turning it over and over, then the others snatched at it too, and took their turns.

Bigman said, "Is that the capsule? Are you sure?"

"I'm reasonably sure. We'll open it, of course, and make certain."

"But, when, how, where——" They were all about him, demanding.

He fended them off. "I'm sorry. I really am. . . . Look, do you remember the few words we picked up from Agent X just before his ship blew up? Remember the syllables 'normal orb,' which we decided meant 'normal orbit'? Well, the Sirians made the natural assumption that 'normal' meant 'usual,' that the capsule would be put into the kind of orbit usual for ring particles, and looked in the rings for it.

"However, 'normal' also means perpendicular. The rings of Saturn move directly west to east, so the capsule in a normal orbit to the rings would move directly north to south, or south to north. This made sense, because then the capsule would not be lost in the rings.

"Now any orbit about Saturn moving directly north and south must pass over the north and south poles, no matter how else that orbit varies. We approached Saturn's south pole and I watched the mass detector for anything that seemed to be in the proper type of orbit. In polar space there were hardly any particles, so I felt I ought to be able to spot it if it were there.

I didn't like to say anything about it, though, because the chances were small, I thought, and I hated to rouse false hopes.

"But something registered on the mass detectors, and I took the chance. I matched velocities and then left the ship. As you guessed later, Bigman, I seized the opportunity to gimmick the Agrav attachment at that time in preparation for the later surrender, but I also picked up the capsule.

"When we landed in Mimas I left it among the air-conditioning coils in Wess's quarters. Then, when we came back to get him and surrender him to Devoure, I picked up the capsule and put it in my pocket. I was routinely searched for weapons when I embarked on the ship, I recall, but the robot searcher did not interpret an inch sphere as a weapon. . . . There are serious drawbacks to using robots. Anyway, that's the whole story."

"But why didn't you tell us?" howled Bigman.

Lucky looked confused. "I meant to. Honestly. But after I first picked up the capsule and got back to the ship, we had already been spotted by the Sirians, remember, and it was a question of getting away. After that, in fact, if you'll think back, there was never one moment when something wasn't popping. I just— somehow—never got around to remembering to tell anyone."

"What a brain," said Bigman contemptuously. "No wonder you don't like to go anywhere without me."

Conway laughed and slapped the small Martian on the back. "That's it, Bigman, take care of the big lug and make sure he knows which way is up."

"Once," said Wess, "you get someone to tell *you* which way is up, of course."

And the ship swirled down through Earth's atmosphere toward landing.

Isaac Asimov

- ☐ BEFORE THE GOLDEN AGE, Book I   C2913   1.95
- ☐ BEFORE THE GOLDEN AGE, Book II   Q2452   1.50
- ☐ BEFORE THE GOLDEN AGE, Book III   Q2525   1.50
- ☐ THE BEST OF ISAAC ASIMOV   23018-X   1.75
- ☐ BUY JUPITER AND OTHER STORIES   23062-7   1.50
- ☐ THE CAVES OF STEEL   Q2858   1.50
- ☐ THE CURRENTS OF SPACE   P2495   1.25
- ☐ EARTH IS ROOM ENOUGH   Q2801   1.50
- ☐ THE END OF ETERNITY   Q2832   1.50
- ☐ THE GODS THEMSELVES   X2883   1.75
- ☐ I, ROBOT   Q2829   1.50
- ☐ THE MARTIAN WAY   23158-5   1.50
- ☐ THE NAKED SUN   22648-4   1.50
- ☐ NIGHTFALL AND OTHER STORIES   23188-7   1.75
- ☐ NINE TOMORROWS   Q2688   1.50
- ☐ PEBBLE IN THE SKY   Q2828   1.50
- ☐ THE STARS, LIKE DUST   Q2780   1.50
- ☐ WHERE DO WE GO FROM HERE?—Ed.   X2849   1.75